"How did you know my first name?"

She looked at him in surprise.

"Doctors know everything," he said, looking mysterious. "Your name is Katherine Elizabeth Logan—Kate for short. You are twenty-six years old, five feet four inches tall, a hundred and three pounds in weight—not counting the five pounds or so you appear to have lost since we last weighed you."

"You've been reading my chart!" Kate exclaimed.

"Of course. You wouldn't want me to treat you without reading it, would you?"

"You didn't prescribe for me, anyhow," Kate accused him.

His face took on a wounded expression. "I most certainly did. I remember exactly what I told you."

"So do I. You told me to go home, take two aspirins, and get some rest."

"As I recall, *you* prescribed the aspirin. *I* prescribed more rest, a nutritious diet, and plenty of exercise. I can see that you ignored my advice, too. The circles under your eyes are worse; you need to gain some weight—which you'll never do if your choice of frozen dinners is a sample of your meals. And from the way you were charging through the supermarket, it's obvious that you haven't eased up on your schedule any."

Kate grinned at him. "But I was getting my exercise."

He threw up his hands in defeat. "I surrender. You're hopeless as a patient. All I can do for you is to see that you get a decent meal. If you'll come into the kitchen and sit at the table, I'll get started on our dinner."

LOVE MORE PRECIOUS

Marilyn Austin

of the Zondervan Publishing House
Grand Rapids, Michigan

A Note From the Author:
I love to hear from my readers! You may correspond with me by writing:

Marilyn Austin
1415 Lake Drive, S.E.
Grand Rapids, MI 49506

LOVE MORE PRECIOUS

Serenade/Serenata is an imprint of Zondervan Publishing House, 1415 Lake Drive, S.E., Grand Rapids, Michigan 49506.

ISBN 0-310-47482-5

All Scripture quotations, unless otherwise noted, are taken from the King James Version of the Bible.

The characters in this book are fictitious. Any similarity to real persons living or dead is a coincidence.

Edited by Ann McMath
Designed by Kim Koning

Printed in the United States of America

86 87 88 89 90 91 92 / 10 9 8 7 6 5 4 3 2 1

To Cindy

CHAPTER 1

KATE LOGAN MANEUVERED HER subcompact through a break in the heavy traffic that clogged the busy North Dallas freeway. Peeling off at one of the towering, mirrored glass buildings that lined the street, she spun into a parking place reserved for the employees of the Hansen Agency, the advertising firm where she worked. The clock on the dashboard of her little blue car warned that in exactly five minutes she was due in the senior executive's office, where she would be expected to present the publicity proposal she had worked up for his newest client.

She stepped from her car, taking a moment to straighten the jacket of her navy linen summer suit and smooth away the wrinkles it had acquired during her hectic race to work. Tucking a bulging portfolio under her arm, she strode rapidly toward the back entrance of the building. Inside, in the suite of offices occupied by the Hansen Agency, she paused at her desk only long enough to glance at her appointment book. She sighed. Already her schedule was full, and the day hadn't even begun.

Distractedly she smoothed her short, dark hair, which was cut to attractively frame a heart-shaped face, brushing back into its proper place a stray lock that was still damp from the August heat. Then, expressive blue eyes reflecting her intense concentration, she set out purposefully for the office of Clint Hansen, the owner-manager of the firm. She didn't bother to check over the ad layouts in her portfolio. There was no need to. Only a few hours had elapsed since she finished them, long after midnight, and their details were still vividly imprinted in her mind.

Clint greeted her with his customary confident smile. "I knew you could do it," he said, reaching for the portfolio. "Let's see what you've got."

Kate handed him the portfolio and watched for his reaction. As he thumbed through its contents, she thought how perfectly Clint fit the image of a successful young advertising executive. Wearing a handsomely fitted, custom-tailored business suit, his thick brown hair fashionably styled, he was a model of suave sophistication. His shrewd gray eyes brightened as he surveyed the layouts she had made.

"Good girl!" He nodded enthusiastically and handed the portfolio back to Kate. "The Qualtech people are going to love this. You've made it sound as though an American home without its very own personal computer is as out of date as a house without electricity. We ought to be able to sell them the complete promotional package, radio spots and all. Just be sure to turn on that pretty smile at lunch today, and we'll have them in our hip pocket."

"I thought they had asked to meet with us first thing this morning," Kate said. "At least that's when they're scheduled according to my appointment book."

"I changed the time."

"But why?" Kate asked in dismay. She was also scheduled to meet with a photographer and interview models for a fashion magazine layout early that afternoon. Now she would be a bundle of nerves during the luncheon meeting for fear she would be late for her afternoon appointment.

Clint arched an eyebrow knowingly. "We're smarter than to try to sell a hungry client, love. We want them well-fed and happy when we make our pitch."

Kate frowned slightly. "That sounds a little calculating, Clint. I'd like to think they'll hire us because they like our work."

"That goes without saying. Just remember that it's your job to answer any questions they may have about the promo package. The selling is my department." He rose from his chair and came around the desk to stand beside Kate. Dropping an arm around her shoulder, he said with a disarming smile, "All you have to do is be your sweet, charming self and explain your ideas to them. I'll do the rest."

Reassured somewhat, Kate relaxed. She was always eager to turn an account over to Clint at this point. Selling was not her strong point. She felt guilty trying to make a client take on more expense than he seemed comfortable with. Clint, on the other hand, smooth and persuasive without ever seeming to be pushy, always managed to manipulate his clients so that they ended up begging to spend more on promotion.

But, as Clint said, sales were his department. And while she might sometimes question his tactics, she couldn't dispute their results. His agency, while undeniably one of the most aggressive in acquiring clients, was equally successful in serving them. Besides, it wasn't her place to be criticizing Clint's methods. She had her own work to do—mountains of it—and she should be spending her efforts on getting it done. It was up to her to meet her crowded schedule, however hectic it might be. After all, its breathtaking pace was what made advertising the exciting business it was, and she loved the heady experience of being a part of it.

She agreed to Clint's plans for lunch and started to leave. But his hand tightened on her shoulder, detaining her. "By the way, I made an important contact at a party last night and lined up a possible new account." He named a local chain of small department stores. "I'm set up to have dinner with some of their executives tonight, and I'd like you to join us so that you can give them an idea of the kind of thing we do. Nothing specific—just a little something that would put us in a talking position with them."

Kate looked ruefully at the portfolio she held, her eyes still burning from the previous night's efforts. "I'm afraid I'll be very poor company—and certainly not very persuasive. I was up half the night working on these."

"I know, and I would have given you more notice if I could. Believe me." A look of intensity came into his eyes and his grip on Kate's shoulder grew tighter. "This could be a big account for us, Kate. I know you can rustle up something to show them."

"I suppose I could try, but there's no way it can be very good," Kate said doubtfully.

"Anything will do. We really don't want to offer them anything specific. Just a bit of whipped cream to give them a taste of what we could do for them. Mostly this is a get-acquainted party." He smiled at her in encouragement. "Consider the evening a reward for your hard work on the Qualtech account."

"I'll see what I can do," Kate said in resignation, "although I can't promise much on such short notice."

"I know you'll come through. You always do," Clint reassured her. He gave her a quick hug before he released her. "By the way, you'll want to look your best tonight. Pick out something special to wear—you know, the 'understated elegance' look you do so well.

Naturally you wouldn't want to outshine the clients' ladies."

"There's little chance of that, the way I'm going to feel," Kate said with a doleful glance at him.

"You'll be perfect—as always." His admiring glance ran over her willowy figure. "Nobody has the flair for style that you do."

"I'll do my best," Kate said, starting for the door.

"That's my girl," Clint called after her. He extended an encouraging smile to her as she left his office.

Back at her desk, Kate regarded its cluttered surface dismally. Her eyes felt grainy from lack of sleep, and her temples were beginning to throb with the beginning of one of the headaches she seemed to be getting more and more frequently these days. There simply weren't enough hours in the day to do all the work Clint assigned her.

As one of the more talented members of his staff, Kate got a large share of assignments. And she wasn't complaining about her heavy workload, which was after all a testimonial to her success at her job. So what if she missed a night's sleep now and then? And certainly an occasional headache was a small price to pay for turning out a really good piece of work. The advertising field wasn't for people who were looking for leisurely paced jobs. It was a fast-moving, competitive business that flirted with failure as precariously as it courted success. It was like riding a roller coaster. If you couldn't take the thrills and spills, you were in the wrong job.

Kate set to work, and the day somehow fell into place. By noon, she was ready for her afternoon appointment. She had also located several samples of successful magazine and newspapers ads which might be adapted for Clint's prospective clients. She stuffed the pages into a briefcase to be studied before she went to dinner that night and, directing her thoughts to the presentation she had prepared for the Qualtech people, took up her portfolio and went to meet Clint Hansen for lunch.

The luncheon meeting went well. With his easy, relaxed charm and self-assured poise, Clint presented Kate's publicity proposal in flawless style, and it was enthusiastically received. They left the luncheon meeting with their client's full approval of the plan and the promise of a generous budget with which to develop it.

On their way back to the office, Clint turned to Kate in jubilation. "We did it! We had them eating out of our hand. They loved our idea."

Kate felt a moment's resentment. She was the one who had originated and developed the idea.

"It wasn't my intention to have anybody eating out of my hand, Clint," she said, unable to completely conceal her irritation. "I only wanted to give our clients an advertising plan they would be happy with."

"And you certainly did," he said in quick acknowledgment.

"Then maybe it was worth losing a night's sleep." Kate rubbed her now throbbing temples. Lack of rest and her rushed morning had combined with the tension-filled luncheon meeting to produce a painful, persistent headache.

Clint cast a sympathetic glance at her. "I know what you're going through, Kate. I've been through it myself. We all have to pay our dues in this business." He patted her hand in understanding. "It won't be like this forever, you know. Just try to hang in there for another year or so, and you'll find yourself with a nice, executive title tacked onto your name."

Kate wanted to cry out that she *was* hanging in there. If she hung in much harder, there wouldn't be anything left of her to promote. But listening to Clint's consoling words, she understood that he was only trying to encourage her. After all, he had been through this demanding period in his career, too. If she wanted to succeed, she had to be willing to pay the price—just as he had. In time she, too, would be rewarded for her hard work and loyalty.

Clint left her at her desk barely in time to make her afternoon appointment. "I'll come by for you about eight this evening," he told her, reminding her with a persuasive smile, "This dinner tonight is important, Kate, so do turn on the charm. And bring along a sample of our work—something impressive. This could be a big-bucks account."

Doggedly, Kate set out for her appointment. Maybe there would be time to think about Clint's department store clients later on. For now, she had all the demands on her time she was able to deal with.

The afternoon appointment went smoothly. Kate was pleased with her session with the photographer. The busy hours took their toll, however. As she threaded her little car through the late afternoon traffic, the headache that had been building all day now pounded painfully, and the blinding summer sun added to her discomfort. If this kept up, there was no way she could entertain clients tonight.

She swung out of the traffic in sudden decision. These headaches were getting to be a nuisance. It was time to stop by her doctor's office and get some help. She couldn't afford to let such an insignificant thing jeopardize her job. There was bound to be some medication he could prescribe that would get her through this evening.

When she reached the office of Dr. Wallace, the physician she usually consulted, she was disappointed to find that he had the afternoon off. His pretty, brown-haired nurse, Rose Stanley, was sympathetic to her plight, though. "Our new associate, Dr. Turner, has some time. I think he can see you if that's satisfactory," she suggested.

"I'd be very grateful," Kate said, relieved. "I

know a silly headache isn't all that important, but there's no way I'm going to get any work done until I get rid of this pain."

"I'm sure you'll find Dr. Turner to be helpful," Rose assured her. "All the patients who have met him like him very much."

Kate discovered the reason for that reaction when she was ushered into Dr. Turner's office a short time later. He looked up from the patient file he was reading to greet her with a smile, and her heart gave a funny little lurch. Dr. Steven Turner could well have traded places with one of the attractive male models who appeared in the agency's ads.

There was a lithe, relaxed grace about his tall figure as he sat on the edge of his desk, swinging one long leg. Golden blond hair curled enticingly over the collar of the open-necked shirt he wore under his white lab jacket. His tanned, even features were just rugged enough to miss being overly handsome. The most remarkable thing about him, though, was his smile. It began at the upturned corners of his mouth to light up his entire countenance and twinkle in the depths of clear, perceptive, topaz eyes.

When he spoke, the effect was even more devastating. His voice was soft and caring, holding a sincere interest as he began the conversation. "Rose tells me you're having a problem with headaches."

Kate took the chair beside his desk and waited while he read her medical record. When he had finished, he looked up at her and said, "These headaches of yours seem to be getting more frequent, Miss Logan."

"I get them when my work piles up," Kate explained. "Usually a warm bath and a good night's sleep takes care of them, but there are times when I just have to keep going. This is one of those times, and I really could use some help. I thought maybe you could prescribe something."

He glanced back at her medical records. "Dr. Wallace notes that you have a stressful job. What kind of work do you do?"

"I work for an advertising agency. We handle magazine, radio, and TV advertising, product and client promotion, that sort of thing."

"That sounds like a responsible job for a woman your age." He studied her speculatively for a moment. "You know, you're a bit young to be having problems with stress. It seems to me that you would be wise to get to the cause of it."

Kate laughed dryly. "That's easy. If I could come up with about six more hours in a day, I wouldn't have a problem."

"Well, since we can't lengthen the day, maybe you need to shorten your work time."

"Unfortunately, that isn't one of my options. When there is work to be done, I have to do it. I should think, being a doctor, you would understand that very well."

He smiled in concession. "True. But regardless of a person's job, she has to keep herself physically fit. The human body is like a finely tuned machine, you know. If it is abused or neglected, it can't function properly."

"I don't abuse my body, Dr. Turner," Kate said, her irritation surfacing. "Not with cigarettes or alcohol or anything else."

"How much exercise do you get?"

"Exercise is the last thing I need," Kate said with a wry half-smile. "My problem is finding time to sit down for a minute."

"How about proper rest and nourishment?" His glance ran over Kate's slender figure. "Not that you aren't well proportioned in weight and height. But do you get a properly balanced diet?"

"Actually, I'm not really all that fussy about food. When it's time to eat, I eat."

The lazy smile reappeared. "If you happen to think about it?"

Kate gave an exasperated sigh. "I suppose. Eating just isn't all that big a thing with me."

"Maybe it should be," he suggested.

Her annoyance flared. "Look, Dr. Turner. I don't have any problem with diet. I've just got a splitting headache which is getting worse. I'm sure you're right in suggesting that I need to get more rest. And I intend to—just as soon as I get my work better organized. But I do have a very important business engagement tonight, and I thought maybe you could give me something to help me through it."

He shook his head. "I can't give you a prescription for anything stronger than what you can buy at a drugstore. Not without a specific diagnosis, and Dr. Wallace seems to have ruled out any serious cause for your headaches."

Kate leveled a cynical glance at him. "In other words, go home and take two aspirins."

"If you want to put it that way. I'm afraid I can't give you any other advice. If you alter your busy schedule and the headaches persist, then I think Dr. Wallace might want to do some tests to be sure we aren't overlooking a more serious condition."

"If I had time to go through a bunch of tests, I wouldn't have a headache," Kate said crossly, jumping to her feet. "It looks as though I've wasted both your time and mine."

"I'm sorry I can't offer you more help, but I have to be guided by my best judgment. And I don't think it's in a patient's best interest to mask symptoms with drugs," he replied, unperturbed. "Unless there is a real need for a medication, I think a healthful program of exercise, good nutrition, and plenty of rest offers a far better treatment."

Kate turned toward the door. "In that case, I had better get home and get started on it."

"I hope you will," he said calmly, ignoring her ill humor. He gave her a conciliatory smile as she marched, stiff-backed, from his office.

Once in her car, Kate gave vent to her irritation, blaming herself for her foolish impulse. She should have known it would be a complete waste of time to see a doctor. And wasn't it just her luck to end up with an exercise and diet freak like Dr. Turner? The man was completely unreasonable. How in the world did he think she was going to find time for leisurely strolls in the park and cooking up health foods when she could barely find time for sleep?

She did follow Dr. Turner's advice, however. And after a leisurely bubble bath and a short nap, her headache had disappeared. Miraculously, too, an idea for a promotion plan came to her while she was dressing. By the time Clint Hansen arrived to take her to dinner, she had even managed to rough out a couple of sketches to demonstrate her concept to their clients.

As a result, the dinner meeting went very well. The clients were enthusiastic about the publicity campaign she outlined, and Clint was ecstatic. Picking up on Kate's idea, he enlarged upon it, arousing an even more positive response. By the end of the evening, they had a commission to begin work on a preliminary proposal.

When she climbed wearily into bed that night, exhausted from the long, demanding day, she felt a deep satisfaction. Somehow she had managed it all—and done well. But as she drifted off to sleep, her last thought was, surprisingly, of young Dr. Turner. Wouldn't he gloat to know he was right about her headache? She hadn't needed any medication after all. Just as he had suggested, a few minutes' rest had done the trick.

Of course, he needn't have been so stuffy about it. Just because she wasn't up at daybreak madly jogging and doing pushups, it didn't mean she was a dissipated wreck. Dr. Turner, she feared sadly, was simply a stick-in-the-mud. Then, remembering the way his hair curled at the nape of his neck and the beguiling little crinkles at the corners of his eyes when he smiled, Katie sighed drowsily. Wasn't it a shame that a man with such a sexy smile had to be absolutely weird on the subject of physical fitness? Because of one thing she was certain: Dr. Turner, health freak, had seen the last of Kate Logan.

CHAPTER 2

KATE'S HEALTH WAS AGAIN a subject for conjecture a few weeks later when Helen Logan stood in front of her daughter's refrigerator, regarding its sparse contents with dismay. She turned to inspect an almost empty cupboard and exclaimed, "I don't want to sound like an overanxious mother, Kate, but I don't see how you survive, living the way you do. There simply isn't anything here to eat. It's no wonder you're so slim that a good, strong puff of wind would blow you away. From the looks of this kitchen, I'm sure you never have a decent meal."

Kate sighed. Her parents had come to the city for an overnight visit, and as always her mother's first stop had been the kitchen. "I'm just a little low on supplies right now," she defended herself. "I've been sort of busy lately and really haven't been eating at home much."

Her mother shook her head in disapproval. "Which means that you eat no breakfast at all, some completely inadequate bit of junk food for lunch, and then whatever is the least trouble for your dinner."

"I eat out most evenings, and I eat very well. I get my share of calories and more. Believe me."

"That's exactly my point," her mother persisted. "While I don't mean to imply that restaurant food is inferior . . ."

"Please don't. One of our best accounts is a chain of restaurants," Kate interrupted with a grin.

"Just the same, there's no substitute for simple, home-cooked food." Helen Logan inspected her daughter with a critical eye. "You have circles under your eyes, too. I can tell you're not getting enough rest. I don't mean to say, 'I told you so,' but this living alone in the city is turning out exactly as I feared it would. This really is no way to live."

Kate listened to her mother patiently. This was an oft-repeated scene between them. Her parents had never been enthusiastic about her move to the city. Yet while she disliked giving them cause for any anxiety, she had stood firm in her decision. She had known since she was in high school that she wanted a career in advertising, and there simply were no such job opportunities in the small town where the Logan family lived.

That their little town was located less than a hundred miles from Dallas did little to bridge the distance between Kate and her parents. With Kate's busy schedule, it was a rare weekend when she was entirely free. Either there was a business-social engagement that Clint Hansen wanted her to attend, or she needed the time to catch up on her work. Her visits to her hometown were usually confined to special holidays and what little vacation time she could manage.

Her parents made up for her lack of time by occasional overnight, spur-of-the-moment visits such as this one. And their visits were always a welcome treat for Kate. There was something solid and reassuring about her father's quiet strength, something comforting about her mother's loving concern. Even her fussing over her daughter's welfare was a pleasant sound to Kate's ears. And not for the world would she have admitted how eagerly she opened the hampers of home-cooked food they always brought. She could only give them an extra-tight hug and hope they understood how very much she loved them.

This visit was no exception. Upon learning that Kate had a free Saturday evening, her parents had loaded up the car and made a quick trip into the city. As always, the time sped by all too quickly. While Kate's mother inspected her wardrobe for signs of neglect, her father took care of the minor repairs to the apartment that always seemed to need doing when he came to visit. The food her mother had prepared tasted better than the finest cuisine Dallas had to offer. The three of them talked late, catching up on family news. Too soon, her father announced that it was past his bedtime.

"I'm not as pretty as my girls. I need my beauty sleep," he joked. "Besides, we'll need to be up early to go to church."

Kate felt a twinge of conscience. In the Logan family, church attendance had always been as much a part of Sunday as the dawning of the day. Yet she no longer seemed to get to services except when her parents came to visit.

She felt the omission keenly the following morning when she was seated between her parents in the sanctuary of the church they always attended when they were in town. It was the loveliest of summer mornings, and the sunlight filtering through stained glass windows cast a jeweled glow over the pulpit. Joining in the familiar hymns they had sung together so many times, Kate felt a sweet nostalgia for those happy Sundays that made up some of the most treasured memories of her childhood.

Sitting beside her father, she felt the never-failing

security she found in his presence, a deep respect for his unfaltering faith, and wonder at the unshakable integrity with which he lived his life. As slight as her own working experience was, she had already learned how difficult it was to maintain the standards of business conduct he lived by. In her business it would be folly to trust to mere verbal agreements. Yet the best legal minds had still to find words that could be as binding as a simple handshake with John Logan. With pride, Kate sat beside him, sharing in the church services. As she observed the kindness in his expression and the serenity in her mother's face, she felt an inexpressible love for these two fine people who set such a worthy example.

The service seemed to last only minutes. Still, Kate left the sanctuary with the greatest sense of well-being. She was chatting happily with her mother when she heard someone call her name. Turning, she saw with surprise that the handsome doctor she had recently visited was walking beside them.

"You're looking very well this morning, Miss Logan. I trust you got over headache," Dr. Turner said, smiling down at her.

With some discomfiture, Kate remembered the unpleasant ending of their previous encounter. She could have sworn she detected a hint of amusement in his smile. She also sensed the curiosity his comment had aroused in her mother, who had stopped and was waiting to be introduced.

Hoping to forestall any questions, she made the introductions hastily. "My parents are visiting me for the weekend," she added in a diversionary tactic.

She was unsuccessful. "Is Kate a patient of yours?" her mother asked, instinctively zoning in on the uncomfortable subject.

Steven Turner glanced at Kate and his smile broadened. "She consults my colleague, Dr. Wallace—although I served as a substitute for him recently." He directed his attention to Kate. "I hope you've had no recurrence of your headache."

"I'm fine. Absolutely fine," Kate replied in a hearty tone. "Actually, it was pointless of me to bother you. By the time I got home, my headache was gone."

"Still, you should consult Dr. Wallace if your headaches continue. I'm afraid I didn't make that clear enough to you. But you did leave my office rather hurriedly." Again, to Kate's irritation, the amusement appeared in his eyes. There was no mistaking his reference to her displeasure with the outcome of her visit.

"I realized I was simply wasting your time—as well as my own," Kate said.

"As I recall, you were on your way to an important appointment. I hope it turned out well for you."

"Very well," Kate said, relieved at the change of subject.

Steven Turner seemed to sense her feelings. He turned to her parents and said politely, "Are you able to visit your daughter often? I don't believe I've seen you at church before. But then, I haven't been coming here all that long myself. I'm something of a newcomer to town."

Kate's mother took up the subject instantly. "We come here as often as we can, and I can't think of a better place to get acquainted. This seems like a very friendly church."

"The minister at my home church recommended it to me. He said this was not only the friendliest church in the city but that it also had the prettiest girls. Naturally, as a lonely bachelor, I made this my first stop when I moved here," he added with an engaging grin.

Kate's mother returned his smile agreeably, obviously taken by his ingratiating candor. "I hope you haven't been disappointed."

"Absolutely not. The longer I come here, the

prettier the girls get." His glance settled on Kate, and she again sensed a teasing edge to his words.

"Then you must be here every time the doors open," she said dryly.

"I do my best." The twinkle in his eyes told Kate he had not missed the barb in her remark. He turned to her parents and chatted a moment longer, ending the conversation by expressing the hope that he would see them at church the next time they were in town. He directed a last remark to Kate. "Perhaps I'll see you in the meantime—at church, of course." His playful tone told her he was fully aware of her disapproval of him as a doctor.

"Of course," Kate said, nodding politely to him as he went on his way.

Her mother, with her usual intuitiveness, picked up on the conversation. She was full of questions as they drove home from church.

"That young doctor, Kate, exactly how did you happen to consult him? He said something about headaches."

"It was nothing, Mom. I just had a busy day and in a weak moment stopped by Dr. Wallace's office to get a prescription. He was out, so I saw Dr. Turner. That's all there was to it."

"Still, I hope you'll follow his advice. I don't think one should take recurring headaches lightly. And clearly he felt the same way." Helen Logan shook her head in concern. "It's the way you live—rushing around and eating the wrong things, never getting any rest."

"I'm fine, Mom," Kate insisted.

Her mother was unconvinced. "I know you think I'm making a fuss over nothing. But you'll find that you pay when you get older for neglecting your health when you're young."

For the rest of the drive home, her mother gave voice to her concerns. Kate silently reproached

Steven Turner for her plight. Had the man never heard of doctor-patient confidentiality? And why did he have to show up at church, of all places? One thing was certain, she would have to be on the verge of death before she ever consulted him again.

The subject of Kate's health had been exhausted by the time the Logan family reached Kate's apartment. Kate's displeasure with Steven Turner was forgotten as they enjoyed the lunch Helen Logan prepared. Unable to resist a second piece of her mother's delicious lemon cake, Kate groaned as she sank down into a lounge chair after the kitchen was tidy and the leftovers put away. The family spent a lazy afternoon, exchanging stories about the happenings at home and Kate's eventful life in the city. All too soon, it was time for her parents to begin their drive home.

While her mother packed up the few things they had brought with them, Kate's father took her aside. His expression was solemn as he said, "You're a grown woman, Kate, and have the right to find your own way. But I wouldn't be a proper father to you if I didn't express my concern for you. I'll admit that your mother tends to be overanxious about you, and I understand that you love your job. I know how satisfying it is to meet such a challenge. But there are things of importance in life besides work."

"I know that, Dad. And believe me, I don't intend to go on indefinitely as I am. When I'm better established, I'll be able to slow down. I hope I'm smart enough to know that I'll burn out if I don't. And my work is too important to me to let that happen."

Her father hesitated and then leveled a discerning glance at her. "There's more to my concern than just your total involvement in your work, Kate. What about all the socializing you seem to be caught up in? Are you sure you can handle it all?"

"Socializing is part of my job, Dad. Our business depends on contacts—keeping up with the old ones and making new ones."

"Your business isn't so different from lots of others in that respect, but your job does appear to make some demands on you that don't seem to me to be entirely necessary," her father commented.

"I do get tired of so much partying, but that's the way Clint believes in doing business."

His eyes remained troubled. "All I'm trying to say in a very clumsy way is that I wonder if it's wise to slip into a way of life that centers entirely around your job and business acquaintances you may not have all that much in common with."

Kate hesitated. "I'll admit that a lot of the people I do business with definitely move in the fast track, but that doesn't mean I have to keep up with them. Or that there aren't plenty of others in the business besides me who don't care for the racy life."

"Of course there are. And it seems to me a mistake not to be a bit discriminating in your choice of associates."

"I don't have all that much choice, Dad. Clint is the one who sets the pace."

"Then maybe you need to do some thinking about Clint's priorities and how willing you are to go along with them. You have a right to save some time to be with people you like simply because they're your kind of people."

"And I will, Dad. Just as soon as I get these first years of work behind me."

"It's easy to get caught up in the competition and the striving for success and forget that there are other important things in life," her father said gently.

"Not me," Kate said stoutly. "You and Mom did too good a job of raising me for that to ever happen."

"It's not that I doubt you, Kate. I know you've got a level head." He offered her a conciliatory smile. "I guess I'm only being a father who doesn't want to accept the fact that his daughter is a grown woman with a will of her own."

"I'll never disappoint you, Dad. I promise," Kate said, giving him a fierce hug.

Her father patted her shoulder self-consciously. "I just don't want you to wear yourself out, Kate. You're the only little girl your mother and I have."

He went to load the car, leaving Kate to a final quick chat with her mother. After Kate bade her parents an affectionate goodbye, she was as always a bit tearful. In spite of her busy life, she missed the happy times they spent together.

She sat for a time in the now silent apartment, thinking over her father's words. She had to admit that more than a few of her acquaintances were people she would never spend her time with, given a choice. Admittedly, too, she often questioned Clint's freehanded, social approach to business. Not all agencies were as fast-paced as his.

But then not many of them were as successful. And it was up to the individual to keep personal standards intact. As Clint reminded her, you had to take business however it came to you and deal with whoever came your way.

But then, you had to learn to judge people carefully and hang onto your values, whatever your path in life. Nobody was going to change her standards, that was for sure. She hated the thought of causing her parents any worry—about her companionships *or* her health.

Of course, if it hadn't been for the chance meeting with one Dr. Turner, the whole subject of her work and health would never have come up. Why, of all the churches in the city, had he picked that particular one to go to? And thanks to his loose tongue, her parents had been upset for nothing. If she hadn't wanted to have as little to do with him as possible, she would have called him on the phone and told him what she thought of his meddling.

By midweek, Kate had forgotten her annoyance with Steven Turner. She had no time for thoughts of small aggravations. She was too busy trying to avoid larger ones as she juggled the conflicting demands of the various accounts she was working on.

On Thursday, she worked late finishing a fashion ad. She had to hurry to get home in time to go out again that evening. A reception was being held by one of the agency's major clients, and both she and Clint had been invited to attend. In the interest of time, Kate was meeting Clint at the reception.

She dressed quickly but carefully, choosing a dress of sky blue chiffon that flattered her dark hair and perfectly matched the vivid blue of her eyes. The dress was styled with a short fluttery skirt; insets of lace framed the neckline and accented long, full sleeves gathered at the wrists. Billowing in a filmy swirl around Kate's slim figure, it was soft and feminine but still comfortable to wear and not overly formal. After a brief check in the mirror, Kate set out for the reception a little after seven o'clock, allowing extra time for possible traffic snarls.

She was soon glad for her foresight. She had driven only a few blocks from her apartment complex when she heard a thumping sound from the left front wheel of her car. The car suddenly developed an alarming wobble. When she pulled over to the curb and got out of the car to inspect the wheel, she saw with sinking heart that the tire was flat.

With exasperation, she regarded the useless tire. There was no way she could change the tire, dressed as she was for a party. It was too late to call Clint and tell him of her plight. The nearest service station was at least a mile away, and its repair department was undoubtedly closed for the night. Besides, in her filmy chiffon dress and flimsy sandals, she was in no way dressed for a long hike. She finally decided that the best thing to do was walk back to her apartment and call a taxi. She felt sure Clint would be able to bring her home.

She was about to lock her car and start walking when she saw a lone jogger approaching. As he drew nearer, she recognized him with dismay. Even in racing shorts and T-shirt, Steven Turner was instantly identifiable. She dreaded seeing him, especially under these unhappy circumstances.

His recognition of her was equally swift. By the time he stopped beside her, he had perceived her predicament. "I see you've got a problem," he said, smiling at her and panting at the same time. "Can I help?"

Kate managed a doleful half-smile. Tempting as his offer was, she felt obligated to refuse it in view of her previous encounters with him. "Thanks," she managed bravely, "but I was just heading back to my apartment to call a taxi."

He regarded her doubtfully, taking in the cocktail dress and delicate sandals. "You're not exactly dressed for walking. And a taxi tonight won't get you to work in the morning. I'll be glad to change the tire for you—that is, if you have a spare."

"Of course I have a spare," she replied, offended by the intimation that she might be less than prudent. "I'm perfectly capable of changing the tire, too, except that I'm hardly dressed for the job."

"Hardly," he agreed, adding hastily, "and I don't for a moment suggest that you're not very capable with a tire iron. Under the circumstances, though, why don't you let me help you out? Who knows? I may have to ask a favor of you sometime."

With his lips curved in a disarming smile and his blond hair curling damply against his forehead, Steven Turner had an undeniable appeal. "Well . . . ," Kate began hesitantly.

Without waiting for her to finish, he opened the trunk of her car and unloaded the tools for changing the tire. He swept aside her protestations and began jacking up the car. "You mentioned walking back to your apartment," he said as he sat cross-legged on the pavement, loosening the lugs on the wheel of the car. "I take it that you live somewhere nearby."

Kate nodded and pointed in the direction of her apartment complex. "In the Waterview down the street."

"Then you're my neighbor. I just moved into the Falls."

The complex he mentioned adjoined the one where Kate lived. "Welcome to the Dead Sea," she said.

He looked at her questioningly. "Should that name mean something to me?"

"That's what the residents call this group of apartment complexes. Every complex has something about water in its name, and except for one little swimming pool in the middle of each unit there's not so much as a fish pond for miles."

He grinned. "I guess we're supposed to depend on our imaginations."

"Or hang pictures in our living rooms depicting waterfalls and lake scenes and the like."

"I hadn't thought of that. I'll have to try it. Maybe my mounted swordfish will do. I had intended to hang it in my office, but under the circumstances it might be more effective in the apartment."

"Definitely. I don't think it suggests quite the right atmosphere for a doctor's office."

After considering her remark for a moment, he asked, "Too frivolous for a doctor?"

She shook her head. "I don't think it plants a positive image in the patients' minds. A tank of tropical fish maybe, but never a mounted swordfish." When he looked at her, baffled, she explained, "Things in a doctor's office ought to be . . . well, you know . . . everything ought to be *alive*."

He threw back his head and laughed heartily. "I see

what you mean. And I thank you for the tip. Definitely, the swordfish will hang in my apartment. I can't afford to risk scaring off any of my patients." He took the flat tire off the car and replaced it with the spare. While he tightened the lugs, he continued his conversation. "Speaking of patients, how is your health? Are you getting more rest and exercise?"

"My health is perfectly fine, Dr. Turner," Kate said. Reminded of her annoyance with him, she added, "I do wish you hadn't brought up the subject with my parents, though. You got them all upset over a simple headache."

His expression became contrite. "I'm sorry. I guess it wasn't very professional of me to mention the matter in their presence."

"It really wasn't," Kate agreed.

"I realized at the time that you were annoyed, and I regretted my blunder. It was just that I was concerned about your well-being."

"I do appreciate your interest," Kate conceded, pacified somewhat by his apology. "But I assure you that I am in very good shape."

Having finished with the tire, he rose to his feet and wiped his hand on the front of his T-shirt. Glancing over Kate's trim figure, he said with an unabashed grin, "Miss Logan, I would say that your shape is excellent."

There was no questioning his meaning or the admiration in his glance. His expression was definitely not that of a physician but of a man interested in a pretty girl. Observing his tanned, athletic body and attractive features, Kate found herself a bit breathless. Before the charm of his smile, she was suddenly at a loss for words.

She was saved an answer when he picked up the flat tire and stowed it in the trunk of the car. Neither of them spoke until he had put away the tools and closed the trunk. Then opening the car door for her, he waited until she was seated behind the wheel to offer a suggestion. "It would be a good idea to get that tire repaired without delay. It's risky to be driving around without a spare."

This time Kate was in no way displeased by his expression of concern. "You really saved my life by coming along when you did," she said gratefully. "I don't know how to thank you properly."

"Just tell your friends you know a doctor who is a lifesaver and give them my office number," he joked.

She laughed. "A small enough return for such a big favor. I really do thank you for changing the tire."

"What else are neighbors for?" He closed the door behind her and stood back so that she could go on her way. "I'm sure I'll be seeing you around," he said before she drove off.

Kate found herself distracted by thoughts of Steven Turner as she resumed her drive to the reception. She wondered what he would think of the reception. She felt sure he would heartily disapprove of the menu with its calorie-laden sauces and pastries—not to mention the abundance of alcoholic beverages. His idea of a good meal would probably be wheat germ and bean sprouts—with maybe a little yogurt thrown in for flavor.

But then, remembering his long-limbed, muscular body and clean-cut features, she thought perhaps it wouldn't be so difficult to stomach the menu if it was the price of having dinner with Steven Turner. He really was a most attractive man—even if he was a bit gone on the subject of physical fitness.

CHAPTER 3

In the days that followed, Kate had no time for thoughts of Steven Turner. Every waking moment was occupied by her work. It seemed that each job she finished successfully brought two more in its place. Clint never seemed to run out of new projects to assign to her.

Not that she was complaining. Clint's preference of her work over that of other staff members was a sign of her success. And it was to be expected that success would bring added responsibilities. Still she found herself more and more pressed to keep up with the mounting demands upon her time.

Her success also had another, less pleasurable effect. Her headaches returned with increasing frequency—along with an aggravating impatience. Often she found herself having to apologize to her co-workers for her short temper. The neverending round of business socializing grew more tedious, and she found it ever more difficult to maintain a cheerful facade.

She knew that both her physical symptoms and her

edgy disposition were a result of being overtired and overworked. Yet knowing the reason for her headaches did nothing to stop them. Nor was there any point in consulting a doctor. Under no circumstances would she have admitted her plight to Steven Turner. She already knew the advice he would give her, and Dr. Wallace would doubtless agree with his young colleague. She settled for trying to relax as best she could by stealing a little time each weekend for a quick swim in the pool at her apartment complex or to at least lie out and sun for a bit on the small balcony that opened off her sitting room. These feeble efforts helped about as much as a strip of adhesive applied to a bleeding wound, of course. All she really accomplished with her half-measures was to confirm that she was very tired.

One evening after a particularly trying day, she stopped at the supermarket near her apartment complex to pick up something for a quick supper. She planned to spend the evening working on copy for an ad layout and wanted the quickest, easiest-to-prepare thing in the store. She picked out a few items from the frozen food department and placed them in her grocery cart. Wheeling the cart around abruptly, she headed back toward the checkout counter. Distracted and in a hurry, she didn't notice that she had turned directly into the path of another cart. There was a resounding crash as the carts collided. A pain shot through her thumb. In reflex she pulled her hand back only to find that it was jammed between the carts. Then as the pain hit full force, she cried out involuntarily.

"Don't try to move your hand. You'll only jam it worse. Let me try to get the carts untangled," she heard a familiar voice say. She looked up to see the concerned face of Steven Turner.

She barely heard his apologies as he freed her injured hand from the carts and examined it. She could scarcely see for the tears that had rushed to her eyes. Gratefully, she permitted him to wrap his handkerchief around the thumb, which had begun to bleed.

"I don't think it's broken or the knuckle jammed. I think it's just badly bruised. But the nail appears to be torn, and that cut ought to be treated." He cast an inquiring glance at her. "If you feel well enough to go through the checkout line, it might be best if we got out of here so that I can take a closer look at it."

Obediently, Kate submitted to his instructions and went with him to the parking lot where her car was parked. He held the door open for her to get into the car and then slid into the driver's seat. When he took her keys from her and started the engine, she asked in surprise, "Where are you taking me?"

"To my office where I can take care of this properly."

"That isn't at all necessary. I'm sure I'll be fine in a few minutes."

He shook his head. "No way. That thumb needs attention. The least I can do is treat it after running into you the way I did." He looked at her apologetically. "I really am sorry, you know. I honestly tried to stop. It was just that you turned so suddenly."

Kate could see that he was genuinely upset. "It wasn't your fault," she reassured him. "I was in a hurry and didn't pay attention to where I was going."

"Just the same I feel really bad about hurting you. Try to hang on until we get to the office. I've got something there that will ease the pain."

The throbbing had intensified as the numbness wore off and, although she would not have admitted it to Steven, Kate was grateful for whatever help he could give her. By the time they reached his office, she was more than ready for the analgesic he applied to relieve the pain.

He worked quickly and gently, and Kate felt

nothing when he clipped away the broken nail and treated her injured thumb. She watched his deft, skillful hands with interest, impressed by their sensitivity. Stealing a glance at his intent face, she found herself admiring his clearly defined profile and the golden gleam of his hair in the bright light of the examining room. It seemed only moments until her thumb was neatly bandaged and the pain eased.

"Remind me to be sure to have all my collisions at the supermarket with doctors," Kate said, wiggling her thumb gingerly.

"Better still, how about trying to avoid collisions altogether?" He put away his instruments and turned back to look at her curiously. "Not to be making excuses for running into you, but where were you going in such a hurry? You were charging through the store like a paramedic on a call."

"I was just in a hurry to get my supper. I've got some important work to do tonight." A distressing thought occurred to Kate. "My frozen dinners! I forgot all about them. They're probably thawed by now."

He shook his head. "I brought them in and put them in the refrigerator here at the office. They should be all right. Although . . ." He hesitated and then ventured a suggestion. "Why don't you let me make dinner for us? Your thumb is going to want to be treated gently for the next twenty-four hours or so. Besides, the least I can do to make up for my carelessness is provide your supper."

"The carelessness was mine," Kate corrected him. "My mind was a million miles away, and I wasn't paying the least attention to what I was doing. I'm just glad I didn't hurt somebody else. I should be doing the apologizing. I'm sure you would like to have had your own dinner ages ago."

"I would much prefer to have it in your company." He took her by the arm, forestalling further objections. Retrieving her frozen dinners from the refrigerator, he closed the office and escorted her to her car.

He drove back to the supermarket and turned in at the apartment complex across the street from it. "This is where I live," he explained.

He was parking her car when Kate caught sight of her bulging briefcase in the back seat. "I ought to get home," she said reluctantly. "I really do have to work tonight."

"The work will wait until you've had something to eat," he insisted.

Kate let herself be persuaded, finding that the longer she was with him, the less pressing her work seemed to be. After all, she thought mutinously, wasn't she entitled to a few minutes of her time to do something simply because she wanted to do it? Suddenly she wanted to have dinner with Dr. Steven Turner very, very much.

His apartment was attractively furnished and neatly kept—not at all what she would have expected a busy bachelor's quarters to be. Although equipped with a minimum of furniture, the pieces were tastefully chosen. She noticed, positioned above a leather upholstered sofa, an impressive mounted swordfish. She turned to her host with a smile. "You really do have a swordfish."

"Of course I do. And you'll notice that I took your advice about not hanging it in my office," he pointed out, smiling back at her. There was an appealing charm in his expression that set Kate's pulses racing, leaving her feeling fluttery and perplexed by her strong reaction to him.

To cover her confusion, she wandered across the room to admire an interestingly grouped collection of black-and-white prints depicting waterfowl of various kinds. She leaned close to admire them, noticing that they were original works—and very good ones. "Why, Dr. Turner, I see you have your very own set of etchings," she teased.

His lips curved into a broad grin. "Naturally. You're looking at your genuine, all-American bachelor pad. And I like my friends to call me Steve."

"I'm not sure I'm much of a friend. So far, about all I've done is cause you trouble."

He shrugged. "I like being a Good Samaritan. Especially for pretty women named Kate."

"How did you know my first name?" she asked in surprise.

"Doctors know everything," he said, looking mysterious. "Your name is Katherine Elizabeth Logan—Kate for short. You are twenty-six years old, five feet four inches tall, a hundred and three pounds in weight—not counting the five pounds or so you appear to have lost since we last weighed you."

"You've been reading my chart!" Kate exclaimed.

"Of course. You wouldn't want me to treat you without reading it, would you?"

"You didn't prescribe for me, anyhow," Kate accused him.

His face took on a wounded expression. "I most certainly did. I remember exactly what I told you."

"So do I. You told me to go home, take two aspirins, and get some rest."

"As I recall, *you* prescribed the aspirin. *I* prescribed more rest, a nutritious diet, and plenty of exercise. I can see that you ignored my advice, too. The circles under your eyes are worse, you need to gain some weight—which you'll never do if your choice of frozen dinners is a sample of your meals. And from the way you were charging through the supermarket, it's obvious that you haven't eased up on your schedule any."

Kate grinned at him. "But I was getting my exercise."

He threw up his hands in defeat. "I surrender. You're hopeless as a patient. Dr. Wallace has my sympathy. All I can do for you is to see that you get a decent meal. If you'll come into the kitchen and sit at the table with your hand elevated to keep your thumb from throbbing, I'll get started on our dinner."

Kate followed him to the kitchen and sat down at the table as she was instructed. He began assembling the ingredients for their meal. She watched, fascinated, as he worked at a chopping board expertly preparing an assortment of fresh vegetables, which he sprinkled with a mixture of herbs, placed in a steamer, and set on the stove to simmer. Next he arranged several fish fillets in a pan, seasoned them with lime juice and more herbs, and put them in the oven to bake. While he waited for the main dishes to cook, he assembled a large salad of lettuce, tomatoes, and freshly sliced mushrooms. Kate's eyes widened when, last of all, he added a handful of bean sprouts and crumbled in a crunchy-looking brown substance.

"Wheat germ. It adds a nice touch," he explained as he tossed the salad. Then he moved to the refrigerator, took out a carton of yogurt, and stirred spices into it.

Kate eyed the mixture suspiciously. "What are you going to do with that?"

"We'll put it on our salads. I think it makes a nice dressing."

"I don't believe this," Kate exclaimed, bursting into laughter.

He looked at her, bewildered. "You don't like yogurt?"

"No. That is, I don't know," Kate managed to blurt out between peals of laughter. "It's just that I told myself a person who had dinner with you would probably get bean sprouts, wheat germ, and yogurt. And that's exactly what I'm getting."

"What's wrong with that?" he asked, looking hurt.

"Nothing. It's just . . ." Kate paused to catch her breath. "You couldn't possibly understand."

"Yes, I do," he replied, affronted. "You think I'm a health food nut."

"Well . . . ," Kate hesitated and then plunged ahead. "You'll have to admit that you really are into this physical fitness bit."

"Of course I am. I'm a doctor. It's my job to try and keep people as healthy as possible."

"I know. It just struck me funny that your dinner would turn out to be exactly what I had expected it would be."

"Laugh all you want, but save your criticism until after you've eaten," he said as he turned to the cupboard to take out plates and cutlery. "In the meantime, use your uninjured hand to set the table."

Kate followed his instructions, and he served their dinner moments later. To her surprise, it was delicious. She ate hungrily, enjoying the last bite of the meal. As she scraped the bottom of her salad bowl, she looked up to see him watching her intently. "Now what do you have to say about my cooking?" he demanded.

"What do we get for dessert?" she replied with a satisfied grin.

In answer, he went to the refrigerator and returned with a bowl of grapes and a wedge of cheese. Watching Kate pop the grapes into her mouth eagerly, he smiled. "Don't try to tell me you didn't enjoy your meal."

"It was heavenly," Kate said, leaning back in her chair, replete. "I take back any derogatory thought or comment I might in my ignorance have made. You are a fantastic cook, Dr. Turner."

"Steve," he corrected.

"Steve, then. And it was almost worth mashing my thumb to be invited to dinner."

"You needn't carry your praise that far, but I'm glad you enjoyed the food. I'll concede that I am perhaps a bit gone on the subject of health. I guess it's because I spend most of my time around people who are sick or hurt." His expression became suddenly serious. "I see so many who are doing their best to cope with illnesses or accidents they've suffered through no fault of their own, and it's very frustrating to be unable to offer them the help I would like to. But even harder to take are the people who have abused their bodies beyond repair."

"I hadn't thought of it that way," Kate said, sobered.

"I'm not trying to sound noble or anything, but I just happen to believe that a healthy body is a gift from God to be treasured and taken care of." He shrugged a bit self-consciously. "I guess that's why I'm a doctor."

"And I expect a very good one," Kate said, subdued. There was a touching humility in his voice, a sincerity in his eyes that made her ashamed of the thoughtlessness with which she had dismissed his efforts to help her.

"I do my humble best, although some of my patients seem to need convincing," he joked in a swift change of mood.

"Patients like me?" Kate asked.

He grinned. "If the description fits . . ."

"I take care of myself," Kate insisted.

"With a proper diet, plenty of rest, and enough exercise?"

"Well, I don't spend a lot of time sitting down."

"But how much time do you spend exercising just for the fun of it?"

Kate cast about for an answer, refusing to admit she couldn't remember the last such occasion. "I swim at the pool in my apartment complex—and I play tennis," she said at last.

"How often?"

"As often as I can," she hedged. "And in spite of what you think, I do watch my diet."

"With frozen dinners?"

"There are worse things to eat."

"Such as bean sprouts and wheat germ?" When Kate couldn't help laughing, he assumed an injured expression. "You're making fun of my cooking again."

"I'm sorry," she said, composing herself. "It was the coincidence of your serving exactly what I had imagined you would have for dinner."

His smile broadened. "Well, at least you imagined having dinner with me. I'll settle for that—even if you do think I'm weird."

Kate's cheeks warmed as she realized she had admitted to a more personal interest than she had intended to reveal. "In any event, you are an excellent chef, and I enjoyed the meal very much," she said lightly. She didn't add that she had also enjoyed the company—which she was finding to be altogether charming. A little too charming, as a matter of fact. Steven Turner, she decided, could definitely be habit-forming.

This was an unsettling thought. Unnerved, she pushed back her chair. "In return for such a fine meal, the least I can do is help with the dishes."

"Absolutely not. First of all, you're wounded and out of action. Second, I never let anybody mess around in my kitchen," Steve said firmly. "I would enjoy a bit of after-dinner conversation, though. And I promise not to mention your health."

Kate hesitated. The offer was decidedly tempting. Then, resolutely, she put the temptation behind her. "I really do have to get home. I have some work that absolutely has to be done tonight."

A hint of disappointment flickered in his topaz eyes, but he nodded and said agreeably, "In that case, I'll take you home—frozen dinners and all."

"You don't need to do that," Kate protested. "I only live a block or so away."

He shook his head. "I wouldn't think of letting a lady go home alone. Besides, you'd do well not to risk bumping that thumb. I'll drive you home."

"But how will you get back to your apartment?"

"I'll jog."

Kate laughed. "I should have known. You know, you really are a physical fitness nut."

"But I'm harmless." He grinned.

Kate wasn't at all sure she agreed with him, considering the rather drastic effect his smile was having on her. Although she permitted him to drive her home without further protest, the nearer they got to her apartment the more reluctant she was to see the evening end. It took the sternest reminder of the pile of papers stuffed in her briefcase to keep her from inviting him in when he accompanied her to her front door.

"In spite of all my teasing, I really did enjoy the evening, Steve," she told him.

"Enough to have dinner with me again?" His voice was soft and persuasive. The dim porchlight silhouetted his features appealingly, and his smile held a compelling charm.

"I'd like that very much," she answered, her heartbeat quickening.

His lips curved into a pleased smile. "I'll make a deal with you. Come by the office after work, and I'll check your thumb. And we can make dinner plans."

"It's a deal," she replied.

"I'll be looking forward to it." He lingered, seeming reluctant to leave. Kate found it impossible to turn away from him. At last he said, "About your thumb, Kate. I'm afraid it's going to be uncomfortable for a day or so."

"Not to worry. I'll do exactly what the doctor ordered," Kate answered. "I'll take two aspirins and call you in the morning."

He laughed softly. "Can I count on that? The part about your calling me?"

"Well, maybe not in the morning."

"Don't wait too long, Kate." His glance traveled

over her face, singling out each feature, and he bent toward her. For a breathtaking moment, she had the impossible thought that he was going to kiss her. Then, with a sigh, he brushed the back of his hand gently against her cheek. "Make that call very soon," he said.

After he had gone, Kate stood for a moment by the door, savoring the memory of the enjoyable evening, thinking how long it had been since she had felt so completely relaxed and carefree. Looking at the briefcase she carried, she pushed it aside defiantly. She wasn't going to spoil such a lovely evening with work. She was going to take Steve's advice and get a good night's sleep.

She tumbled into bed, snuggling down comfortably in spite of her sore thumb. Her doctor would be pleased to know that she had followed his instructions. She was drifting off to sleep when it occurred to her that maybe she ought to consider his other suggestions. Maybe she should do something about the frantic pace of her life. She wasn't going to be any good to herself or anybody else if she burned herself out by overworking.

The thought led to another, sobering question. Could it be that she was making a mistake in the course she was pursuing? Could it be that she was too intent on advancing her career? Would she look back later and wish she had saved some time for her personal life? Would she regret the price she paid for her success?

CHAPTER 4

KATE WAS UP AT DAWN the following morning, refreshed by a full night's sleep. Even though her injured thumb was a sore reminder of her accident the previous evening, her high spirits made up for the discomfort. Eager to begin her work, she arrived at the office early. By the time her morning appointments began, she had managed to complete the work she had planned to do the night before.

Looking at her neatly bandaged thumb, she permitted herself a gratifying recollection of the events of the previous evening. Visions of Steve's appealing smile drifted through her thoughts, stirring a pleasurable anticipation. Her hand reached for the telephone. After all, he *had* asked her to call him and tell him how she was feeling. She smiled, indulging in a moment's further fancy. What would he say if she called and told him she simply couldn't get him out of her mind?

She was visualizing his reaction when she was jolted from her reverie by an insistent voice. "Earth to Kate. Do you read me, Kate? If you're getting my signal, beam down an answer from wherever you are in outer space."

Clint looked down at her in amusement. Kate apologized. "I'm sorry. I guess my mind was a million miles away."

"I'm not complaining. I love to see my people busy churning out ideas," he joked. "It's helpful, though, if they tune back in from time to time so I'll know what they're up to."

Kate thought perhaps he wouldn't be smiling so broadly if he knew her thoughts, but she managed an agreeable smile and answered, "I was going over the revised copy for Le Boutique's fashion layout. I was going to bring it in later for your approval."

He nodded absently. Already his mind had shifted gears. "Then you're ready for another assignment. That's what I stopped to talk to you about," he said. "Come along to my office, and I'll tell you what I've got in mind."

In his office, Clint sat down at his desk and leaned back in his swivel chair to smile up at her triumphantly. "I think I've hooked a really big fish, Kate. I'm counting on you to help me land him."

Kate said nothing, knowing from Clint's pleased expression that he was savoring this moment. He had undoubtedly turned up a possible new account that was very important and wanted the pleasure of revealing his accomplishment in his own time and own way.

"Aren't you the least bit interested?" he asked after a moment, watching her playfully.

"I'm holding my breath in suspense," Kate reassured him.

"Then, since we can't have you turning blue, I guess I'll let you in on the news." He paused to beam at her proudly. "What would you say if I told you there is a very good chance of our signing up Jason Enterprises?"

Kate's eyes widened. Even for Clint, this would be a master stroke. Jason Enterprises was the locally based parent company for dozens of subsidiaries whose interests ranged from real estate development, hotels, and shopping centers to data processing and investment companies. An account such as this was an agency's dream.

"However did you manage it?" she gasped in admiration.

"Just by knowing the right people and being on the spot at the right moment. And, of course, by being able to show that we get the kind of results the Jason people demand." His eyes narrowed, their expression sharpening. "This could be the big one, Kate. The one that could put us in competition with the top agencies. It will take a real effort to sell the Jason people, but I think we can do it if we give it our best shot. And of course I'm depending heavily on your help."

"You know I'll do my very best," Kate promised.

"You can begin tonight. The Jason public relations people have agreed to meet with us at dinner. It will be a purely social evening, of course, but it should give us a chance to get a measure of what it will take to land the account." Clint leaned forward for emphasis. "Naturally, we'll want to put our best foot forward and make the most of the opportunity to impress them."

Quickly, he outlined his plans. "I'm putting together a team of our staff members whose expertise should cover all the areas of the Jason interests. I'd like you to be responsible for their leisure-oriented holdings—hotels and resorts, that sort of thing. You'll get a list later on this morning. I want you to be thoroughly familiar with it so that you can talk to the Jason people knowledgeably tonight."

"That's a tall order," Kate said doubtfully. "I've got a jam-packed day already."

"Then rearrange your day, and drop everything that isn't absolutely necessary. Our dinner with the Jason people has first priority. I don't have to tell you how important it is that things go smoothly tonight." He broke off as he noticed Kate's bandaged thumb. "I hope you can do something about that bandage. It's terribly distracting. What in the world did you do to yourself, anyway?"

"I mangled my finger between two shopping carts at the supermarket."

"Well, keep it out of sight. It does stand out."

"The proverbial sore thumb?" Kate said with a grin.

He frowned. "Maybe you should wear something with long sleeves, something that doesn't call attention to your hands. The impression we make is important."

"I doubt that something as insignificant as my bandaged thumb is going to sully our image," Kate joked.

Clint did not smile. "At this level, no detail is insignificant. It's vital that we project an image of capability and self-confidence."

It was Kate's opinion that Clint put far too much emphasis on surface appearances. She was convinced that a businesslike presentation of quality work was in the long run the most effective approach to clients. Clint, however, insisted that the name of the game was contacts, and spared no expense or effort in his pursuit of them. His present preoccupation underscored his eagerness to land the Jason account. "Maybe I should stay home," she suggested. "I might not be at my best. This thumb could get painful tonight."

He shook his head impatiently. "Absolutely not. We need your input. Take something for the pain and come, but try not to call attention to your thumb. We don't want you coming on as an air-head."

"Thanks a lot," Kate exclaimed, annoyed by his lack of sympathy.

He brushed aside her irritation. "You know what I mean. Naturally, I'm sorry you hurt yourself, but neither of us has time to stand around commiserating. We'll have all we can do to prepare for tonight."

Kate had to agree with him on that score. She hurried back to her desk to reschedule her day. It was going to be difficult, but this wasn't a time to quibble with Clint. He was rarely this openly demanding. Usually, he masked his orders with a suave persuasiveness. His abruptness today was an indication of his anxiety concerning the Jason account.

Diligently following Clint's instructions, Kate appeared at the Club promptly that evening, well-briefed and, she hoped, suitably costumed for the dinner with the Jason representatives. She wore an elegant but conservative dinner suit of brocaded silk in a deep shade of aquamarine that complemented her dark hair.

Clint's earlier nervousness was undetectable as he performed his role of host. Always adept in social relationships with clients, he was at his very best tonight. From its beginning, the evening was an unqualified success.

No detail had been overlooked in providing the guests with a splendid evening. The service was flawless, the setting enchanting, the dinner an exotic offering from a renowned chef. There was a delicious chilled artichoke soup, tender medallions of veal with an assortment of flavorful vegetables, a piquant salad tossed with warm goat cheese, and a delectable white chocolate mousse with raspberries. Each course was accompanied by a fine imported wine.

And yet, though the guests were affable and charming, the conversation witty and entertaining, and the meal an epicurean delight, Kate found herself having to work to enjoy herself. The gaiety seemed to her somehow artificial, so much rich food an overindulgence. She could eat only a part of most of the dishes. Having no taste for wine, she left her glass untouched.

Too, though she did her best to conceal it, she couldn't completely suppress a feeling of impatience. All this festivity was but a facade. The real purpose of the occasion was the agency's pursuit of a lucrative contract, and she would far rather have spent this time and effort telling these people what the agency could do for them. In the end, the contract would be won or lost not on exotic food and lavish entertainment but on the quality of work the Hansen Agency could deliver.

She also found herself comparing the evening to the one she had spent the night before with Steve Turner, wondering how he would react to this sumptuous banquet. She felt certain he would look askance at the rich foods on the menu and, given the chance, would probably have the guests jog around the table to work off the effects of their overindulgence. The thought brought a smile to her lips.

A remark from the woman who sat beside her claimed her attention then, and she guiltily put Steve Turner out of her thoughts. This was no time for fancies about her individualistic doctor, however appealing they might be. She had to be mindful of the serious purpose behind the evening's festivities. Regardless of her personal opinion of Clint's approach, she had to concede that he was no fool where business was concerned. He hadn't gained his success wasting his time on unnecessary effort. When the time came he would be just as diligent in demanding the best work his staff could offer. In the meantime, whether it suited her preference or not, this was the way the agency's business was done.

Sternly, she disciplined her thoughts and set about the task before her. She was not here to approve or disapprove Clint's business methods. Nor, for that matter, was she here to enjoy herself. She was here to do the job Clint had assigned her.

Apparently, Kate's efforts were successful, because Clint stopped by her desk the next morning full of praise for her. "You did a great selling job on the Jason people, Kate. You really came across."

"I hope so. The Jason account would be a dream to work on."

His lips curved into a wide grin. "Then get busy and see what you can come up with. They've agreed to let us work up a presentation for them."

Kate exclaimed with delight. "For certain?"

"For certain. I got a go-ahead from them this morning."

"I can't believe it!" Kate cried out, whirling her chair around in exultation.

"Well, it's true, so we've got to get moving. This presentation has to be the best we can do. I want the full treatment—film clips of the most successful things we've done in the past and a full range of treatments and ideas tailored to the Jason interests."

"How long do we have to do the workup?"

"The sooner we get back to them, the better. But we don't want to sacrifice quality. I'd like to have a staff meeting next week after we've had time to do some preliminary research. At that time, we can set up a schedule and decide on our approach."

Clint's news set Kate's thoughts to racing, and she plunged eagerly into her assignment. This piece of work had to be the best thing she had ever done. She reorganized her schedule, freeing up the maximum amount of time, and began a thorough research of the Jason enterprises she was responsible for.

Caught up in her task, she barely noticed the days speeding by. She was astonished when Friday arrived and the work week was over. Still, it was with relief that she left her office at the end of the day. Her briefcase was loaded with information on the Jason interests, and she planned to spend the weekend studying the file.

At home, she put a frozen dinner in the microwave while she unpacked her briefcase. But she had barely begun sorting its contents when the telephone rang. She answered a bit impatiently, hoping that Clint was not calling with some social demand. She wanted no distractions to interfere with her work.

Her impatience vanished at the sound of the voice that came over the line. "You are a terrible patient," Steve Turner accused her. "You were supposed to come by the office so I could check on your injured thumb."

"I'm so sorry, I forgot all about it," Kate exclaimed apologetically. "I've been so busy I haven't had a free minute."

"I'm amazed you were able to forget. As badly as that nail was torn, I expected you to have a good deal of pain."

Kate chuckled. "I had a good doctor."

"Flattery will get you nothing except an infected thumb," he chided her. "Why didn't you call me as you were supposed to?"

"I honestly never thought of it. My thumb hasn't bothered me at all."

"Still, it should be checked and the bandage changed." He sighed. "You know, I hate to be accused of ambulance chasing, but I expect I had better come by and take a look at you. I can't have my professional reputation tarnished by a neglectful patient."

"I'm sorry," Kate said, contrite. "I didn't mean to be a bother."

"You're not a bother. You're more of a distraction. I can't seem to corner you long enough to treat you. However, being a persistent soul, since the patient won't come to the doctor, the doctor will come to the patient. I'll be over in a few minutes." Before Kate could answer, he broke off the connection.

Kate looked absently at the telephone for a moment. Then she made a dash for her bedroom. She couldn't let Steve see her all rumpled and disheveled. She looked an absolute fright.

By the time Steve arrived, she had brushed her hair and changed into a fresh blouse and comfortable slacks. She was frantically scooping up the clutter of papers that littered the living room coffee table when the doorbell rang.

She opened the door to find him lounging indolently against the door facing, black leather bag in hand. As he looked down at her, his lips curved into a roguish grin. "You're impossible," he told her, "but you're much too pretty to scold. What am I going to do about you?"

"I guess you could come in and look at my thumb," Kate said, returning his smile. "We can't have you wasting a trip."

As he entered the room, a wave of pleasure swept over Kate. His blond hair was brighter, his golden brown eyes even more compelling than she remembered them. She took a deep breath to subdue her quickening pulse and said in a teasing tone, "You're some doctor. I didn't know there were any left who made housecalls. Are you this attentive to all your patients?"

He shook his head. "I refuse to answer on grounds of self-incrimination. I'll only say that it depends on the circumstances—and the patient. Now, go sit on the sofa and let me see if you've still got a thumb."

Kate obeyed meekly. He sat down beside her, opened his bag, and moved immediately to his task. He frowned in disapproval as he began to unroll the bandage on her thumb. "Just what I was afraid of. It's stuck. This is what I wanted to avoid."

Apprehensively, Kate studied her thumb. "Is it going to hurt?"

"Probably." He opened his bag and took out a bottle of some unidentifiable solution. "This may help a little."

He poured some of the solution onto the bandage, saturating it. "It stings," Kate exclaimed in concern.

"The price of neglect," he replied, unmoved. "Let that soak while I go wash my hands."

He returned shortly to resume his ministrations. "I'm not all that great about pain," Kate fretted as he painstakingly worked the bandage loose. She held her breath, flinching against a stab of pain that never came, so deftly did he remove the last bit of gauze. Fascinated, she watched him work, marveling at his gentle hands. By the time he finished rebandaging her thumb, she was intensely aware of his fingers on hers and of the accelerated pounding of her heart. She wondered with some concern if he was as aware of her racing pulse as she was. Still she was disappointed when he released her hand and began replacing the items he had taken from his bag.

"I do apologize for being so neglectful. I know I should have come by your office as you instructed," she said after a moment.

He shrugged. "You're the one who has to bear the cost of the neglect. You're going to pay dearly for this housecall, you know."

"Oh." Kate's spirits plummeted. "Of course, your fee. I realize your time is valuable. It's only right that you should be properly compensated."

"I'm glad you feel that way, because I'm expensive," he said matter-of-factly.

"Naturally." Kate tried to conceal her growing disappointment as she rose from the sofa. "I'll get my checkbook."

"I'm afraid a check won't do."

"I'm not sure I have enough cash. I really don't carry a lot," Kate said, perplexed.

"I can't take cash," he said, eyeing her steadily.
"Then exactly how do you want this handled?" Kate demanded, annoyed.
"I'll settle for taking you out to dinner."
Kate gazed at him, nonplussed. "I don't understand."
His eyes crinkled into an impish smile. "I warned you I was expensive."
A pleasurable relief stole over Kate. Her lips curved into a teasing smile. "Then it should be I who takes you to dinner."
"Unacceptable. I take you, and I get to choose the time and place."
Kate sighed with a feigned resignation. "As your debtor, I suppose I have no choice."
"None whatsoever."
"Then I accept."
"Wise of you. I'll come by for you tomorrow night at seven-thirty."
He picked up his bag and turned toward the door, but Kate interrupted his departure. "Don't I get to know where we're going?"
"It's to be a surprise."
"But how will I know what to wear?" she objected.
He studied the matter for a moment. "I don't like divulging my plans, but I suppose you're entitled to a hint. You can dress for candlelight and atmosphere. I'm taking you to my favorite restaurant."
It was only after he had gone that Kate remembered her plans for the weekend, regarding with dismay the stack of magazines she had intended to study. She decided with some concern that Steve was definitely becoming a threat. How was she supposed to accomplish anything if he kept showing up to distract her?

It took a good bit of effort, but Kate managed to keep her thoughts from straying to Steve as she concentrated on her work the following day. Reminding herself that her evening with him was to be a reward for a day's work well done, she was able to accomplish a respectable quota.

Choosing her costume for the evening was a more difficult task. Usually, dressing for an evening out was a routine matter for her, but tonight she couldn't seem to make a satisfactory choice. She discarded one dress after another, condemning it for fit or unsuitability until she was totally out of sorts. A person would think from the way she was behaving that she had never been to a restaurant before.

Finally she decided on a simple silk dress with a softly gathered skirt and fluttery cap sleeves that called attention to a suggestion of a summer tan. In a delicate shade of shell pink, the material nicely complemented the blue of her eyes. She fluffed her hair with a final twirl of a brush just as the doorbell rang, announcing Steve's arrival.

The restaurant turned out to be the surprise Steve had promised. It was tucked away in the corner of a nearby shopping center away from the concentration of elegant restaurants in more fashionable parts of town. Its exterior was undistinguished. Yet inside, hidden behind the short café curtains that adorned high casement widows, was a delightful little Italian retreat. Red checked cloths covered candlelit tables; romantic Italian music played softly in the background. The spicy aroma of simmering sauces set taste buds tingling.

"If the food is as good as it smells, it must be fabulous," Kate commented as they were seated at their table.

"It is. You get real, home-cooked Italian food when you come here. The Carelli family has operated this place for years. They're really fine people. I met them when Mama Carelli came in for treatment a few months ago." Steve chuckled. "She hadn't been to a doctor since her last child was born, and the whole family had to come with her before she would agree to be treated. Would you believe that eight people crowded into my office?"

"Counting you?"

"In addition to. It was quite a gathering. I haven't had so many people observing me since I was an intern."

"I take it your treatment was successful."

"Luckily for all concerned. Otherwise, I might have had a bit of trouble coping with eight irate Carellis. Especially since none of them had ever heard of me before."

"How did they happen to come to you?"

"Rose Stanley, our office nurse, is a regular customer here. Mama Carelli's finger was badly infected from an imbedded sliver of glass, and Rose convinced her to come and see me. Fortunately, I was able to treat her finger without hurting her."

"You have a gentle touch," Kate said, remembering her own injured finger.

"I'm glad you think so." A twinkle appeared in his eyes, reminding Kate of her startling reaction to that touch. She looked away quickly, disconcerted. To her relief, their waitress appeared at that moment, interrupting the conversation that had suddenly become too personal.

The waitress was one of the Carelli daughters. It was evident, from her cordial response to Steve, that he was an honored guest at their restaurant, and he left the selection of their meal to her. His wisdom was confirmed when the food was served. Kate thought she had never eaten anything quite so delicious. They were served a perfectly seasoned scampi for an appetizer. The main dish was a savory concoction of tender veal, prosciutto ham, and eggplant accompanied by crusty home-baked bread and a salad tossed with Mama Carelli's special vinegar and oil dressing. The meal was topped off with a serving of rich Italian ice cream and espresso coffee.

Kate sighed with contentment as she finished the last spoonful of ice cream. "This food is fabulous," she told Steve. "I don't know when I've enjoyed anything so much."

Steve smiled at her, pleased. "That was the idea. I'll be sure to tell Mama Carelli. She considers it her mission in life to see that people are well fed."

Anna Carelli appeared then to remove their dessert plates, giving Steve his chance to express their appreciation for the fine meal. "Mama will be pleased. Only the best is good enough for Dr. Turner. He's our family doctor, you know," she explained proudly to Kate.

"He's my doctor, too," Kate told her.

"Then you are very lucky." Anna's glance swept over Kate, assessing her. Kate decided that Anna was making a judgment as to whether she measured up to the Carelli's idea of a suitable companion for Dr. Turner. Apparently she passed the test because Anna nodded and said to Steve with a broad smile, "You must bring your friend in again. We promise you another good meal. For now, stay awhile, listen to the music, and enjoy yourselves."

After she had left them to their coffee, Steve leaned forward to study Kate closely. "I'm pleased to hear that you claim me as your doctor. As I recall, you didn't think much of the idea at first. Have you changed your mind about me, Kate?"

The candlelight played across his face, accenting his features appealingly. Kate's breath caught in her throat. "I don't think I ever really had to change my mind," she murmured.

He reached across the table to cover her hand with his. "I hope that means I meet with your approval. Your opinion is very important to me," he said softly.

His touch produced a warm feeling of pleasure, and Kate's hand curved into his. She asked herself with wonder how she had ever thought she could dislike this intriguing man. There was an enchantment in being with him, a wonderful feeling of contentment. She lost all consciousness of time as they lingered over coffee, finding ever new topics of conversation.

It seemed that only moments had passed when they stood outside her apartment door at the end of the evening, lingering, neither of them willing to say goodnight. "It has been a wonderful evening, Kate. I hope you've enjoyed it as much as I have," Steve said softly.

"It was perfect," she hastened to assure him.

"Even though I pretty much forced you into it?"

"You didn't force me into anything. I wanted to come."

"I'm glad to hear that, because I've run out of excuses for seeing you. And I want very much to see you again."

"I'd like that, Steve," Kate answered.

"Then spend the day with me tomorrow. We could go to church in the morning and afterwards go to lunch. There's a place I'd like to take you. I'm sure you'd enjoy it."

"I'd love to go," Kate answered eagerly, delighted by the prospect of being with him again.

He hesitated, seeming to want to say something more, reaching out to take her hands in his. As his fingers clasped hers and raised them to his lips, Kate swayed toward him, wanting instinctively to move into his arms. But instead he bent his head and gently kissed the palm of her hand. "It's going to seem a terribly long time until tomorrow, Kate," he whispered.

When he had gone, Kate lingered by the door, senses reeling, the palm of her hand still tingling from his kiss. Slowly reality returned to her, leaving her bewildered by the effect this man had on her.

What was it about Steve that caused her to lose all reason, to forget all about her responsibilities? She had no business agreeing to spend the day with him tomorrow. No business at all. She was surely taking leave of her senses to even consider it. At a time like this, when her attention to her job was crucial, she couldn't go flitting off and wasting precious time.

Firmly, she resolved to get her emotions in hand along with her priorities. She would go to church with Steve as she had promised, but that was all. Spending the rest of the day with him was out of the question. She would simply explain to him that her work was at a critical point and she couldn't neglect it. For the time being, it had to take precedence over personal affairs. If there was to be any kind of relationship between them, he had to understand her commitment to her career. Tomorrow, she would make it clear to him.

CHAPTER 5

SUNDAY MORNING DAWNED FAIR and bright, a splendid, golden-hued early fall day. Kate sprang from bed eagerly, wanting to have plenty of time to dress for her outing with Steve. She took extra pains with her hair, dawdled over the choice of a dress, examining herself critically when her efforts were at last completed.

She was pleased to see that her hair was behaving nicely. Thick, and glossy dark brown, it was cut in a short, easy-to-keep style that needed only the sweep of a brush to shape it about her face. Her wheat-colored linen dress was appropriately styled to wear to church yet designed for comfort in the warmth of a Texas September. There was an extra sparkle in her eyes this morning, a special glow to her complexion. She felt a luxurious well-being in the prospect of this lovely day.

Or was it, perhaps, the prospect of being with Steve Turner? She had to admit to an uncommon eagerness to see him. Try as she might, she had been unable to shake off the effect of the previous evening. There had been a magic in it that still held her captive, and she could not suppress a thrill of excitement in anticipation of seeing Steve again.

At the thought, she admonished herself sternly. This kind of pointless fancy had to stop. She couldn't permit herself to become emotionally involved. Not now, when her whole future was at stake. Doing a good job right now could determine the entire course of her career, and she had to put a stop to this thing that was happening to her before it got out of hand. She couldn't afford the luxury of a personal relationship with anybody, not even Steven Turner, however tempting the prospect might be.

When Steve arrived a short time later, Kate met him with a firm resolution. She would explain to him that she would go to church with him, but that was all. Afterwards, she would have to come directly home and get to work.

At the sight of him, however, her determination faltered. Her resolve melted instantly beneath the warmth of his smile. This morning, he was even more appealing than she remembered in a blue blazer that accented his broad shoulders and lean height. His clear, topaz eyes sparkled with high spirits and his smooth, tanned complexion held a healthy glow.

His glance rested on her with approval as he guided her to his car. "You look even prettier in the morning sunshine than you do by moonlight," he told her. "You also look as though you rested very well."

Kate wondered what he would say if she told him that, as a matter of fact, her rest was seriously disturbed by dreams of a handsome young doctor. But thinking better of it, she settled for a noncommittal nod and allowed him to seat her in his car.

"I love attending church on Sunday mornings," he said as he drove. "Each Sunday is a beginning. It's as though I'm starting over with a fresh, clean slate that's never been written on before."

"I hadn't thought about it that way, but if it means you get to erase your mistakes and start over, I'm all for it."

He cast an amused glance at her. "Somehow I doubt that you have that many to erase."

"I'm surprised to hear you say that, the way you're always after me to mend my ways."

"It isn't what you do, it's what you *don't* do that concerns me."

"Then I'm in big trouble," Kate grinned. "There are simply multitudes of things I don't do."

"I know, but I can only do so much to help you," he said, shaking his head in mock despair. "I intend to concentrate on seeing that you take time to enjoy life and spend more time with me. The rest of it you'll have to work out for yourself."

Kate smiled, pleased by the idea. "You're a bad influence, Dr. Turner. You're forever trying to undermine my good intentions and lure me away from the things I ought to be doing. You know that, don't you?"

He chuckled softly. "You can't blame a guy for looking out for his own interests."

"But what about my interests?" Kate challenged him.

"I was hoping our interests were the same," he replied, casting a sidelong glance at Kate that left her breathless and a bit disconcerted. What was there about this man that had such a disturbing effect on her?

Fortunately, they turned in at the church parking lot at that moment, saving her a reply. Once inside the sanctuary, she felt all her conflicting emotions subside. Taking part in the familiar services, joining Steve in the hymns she had sung as a child, all her cares and concerns drifted away. A sweet serenity stole over her as they shared an experience that was ever wondrous and new.

Kate left church happy and fulfilled. When Steve set out for the restaurant where they were to lunch, she made no objection. Her only thoughts were of the contentment of the moment.

Their drive took them beyond the outskirts of the city to a charming country inn set back some distance from the highway. Shaded by tall oak and maple trees, it presented an inviting retreat. Walkways led from its terrace to a small, shady pond where ducks and geese swam lazily. The lightly wooded, rolling countryside spread out beyond.

"This is a beautiful place, Steve," Kate exclaimed when they were seated beside a large picture window which overlooked the lovely scene.

"I hoped you would like it. It seemed like a perfect place for a leisurely Sunday lunch."

"How did you ever find it?"

"Rose Stanley told me about it. She comes here from time to time."

"Rose seems to know about all sorts of interesting places. As I recall, she introduced you to the Carelli family restaurant."

"Rose is an irrefutable source of information, as well as an excellent nurse. Dr. Wallace and I would be pressed to get along without her."

"How did you happen to join Dr. Wallace in his practice?" Kate asked, suddenly realizing how very little she knew about Steve.

"He is a longtime family friend who encouraged my interest in medicine. I finished my residency about the time he was ready to cut back on his practice, and he asked me to come in with him. Naturally, I jumped at the chance. He is a very dedicated doctor—as well as a very fine man. I always looked up to him as the sort of doctor I wanted to be."

"Have you always wanted to be a doctor?" Kate asked, curious about the little boy Steve had been.

He nodded. "I was forever bandaging up the

neighborhood cats and dogs, whether they needed it or not."

Kate smiled. "Even then you were beset by reluctant patients?"

"I'm afraid so. There must be something lacking in my patient rapport."

"Not at all," Kate said quickly. "You're the kind of doctor a patient instinctively trusts."

He grinned. "Does that include you?"

"Of course it does. I think you're a fine doctor."

"Then why do you ignore my advice?"

"Because I'm a bad patient. And I don't intend to get drawn into another discussion of that subject," Kate pronounced, picking up the menu.

"A wise decision," Steve agreed. "I'd much rather we ordered lunch. I think you'll find the food a real treat."

The meal turned out to be as special as Steve had predicted, reminding Kate of the delicious Sunday dinners her mother served. She feasted unashamedly on the tender roast beef flanked by delicately flavored vegetables, the home-baked bread still warm from the oven, the flaky-crusted apple pie.

"I feel absolutely sinful to have enjoyed that apple pie so much," she confided to Steve as they strolled beside the pond after lunch. "You're a truly corrupting influence, you know. If I keep hanging out with you, I'm going to be bulging out of my clothes, not to mention looking for another job."

He cast a puzzled glance at her. "What has hanging out with me got to do with your job?"

"I was supposed to spend this afternoon working, but after pigging out the way I did, I feel too lazy to work."

"If getting you to take an afternoon off is corrupting, then I plead guilty. It will do you good to relax and enjoy yourself for a few hours."

Kate shook her head. "It might some other time,

but not this weekend. I'm working on the most important assignment I've ever had."

He walked along beside her silently for a moment, his expression thoughtful. "Is it necessary to spend every moment working, Kate? Do you have to work so hard?"

"I love my work, and I want to succeed at it, Steve."

"But what will it take for you to feel successful? How much work will be enough?"

Finding the question impossible to answer, Kate thrust it aside impatiently. "However much it takes to do a good job, I guess. I don't go around counting the hours. And I definitely don't want to think about them now. If I'm going to goof off an afternoon, I want to enjoy it," she said in sudden decision. Rejecting her earlier intentions, she abandoned the confusing subject and gave her attention to the fat, white geese that waddled alongside the pond. It was too beautiful a day to be squandered on pointless discussion.

Steve joined her at the edge of the pond, and they were soon surrounded by ducks and geese who greedily begged for the crusts of bread they had saved from their lunch. When the bread was gone, Kate and Steve resumed their leisurely stroll. Caught up in the pleasure of the moment, Kate forgot work. There seemed to be nothing more important than enjoying the beauty of this lovely fall day.

They idled away the afternoon with a leisurely drive in the country. The shadows were lengthening into twilight when they at last returned to the city. Relaxed and contented, Kate found herself unwilling for the pleasurable day to end. As they neared her apartment, she suggested on impulse, "I haven't forgotten that I owe you a dinner invitation, and I want you to know that I am not completely without resources where food is concerned. If you'd be interested, I'd like to treat you to one of my favorite meals."

"This I've got to see," Steve said with a grin.

"Don't be condescending. Just take a left at the next corner," she directed.

He followed her instructions, arriving eventually at a small frame house tucked in the middle of a row of shops. Above the narrow doorway was a bright yellow sign bearing a single title: *Li's*. Insisting that Steve wait in the car while she accomplish her mission, she hurried into the store to return shortly with a white paper bag.

She refused to satisfy Steve's curiosity about the contents of the bag during the drive home and made him wait in the living room while she completed the preparations for their supper. Then, with a flourish, she ushered him to the dining table.

The table was set with white bone china and laid with a dark blue tablecloth and matching linen napkins. Blue candles flickered in crystal holders. In the center of the table, flanked by a selection of sauces, rested a platter heaped high with a mound of crispy pastries.

"Egg rolls!" Steve exclaimed as he identified the offerings of the platter.

"The best in town,"Kate announced proudly.

A short time later, surveying the empty platter, Steve voiced his agreement. "I don't think I've ever tasted egg rolls as good as those. How did you find out about them?"

"People who don't have time to cook have built-in sensors that lead them to places like Li's." Kate replied. "Actually, I stumbled onto the place one day when I got lost while I was on an assignment. I was looking for a karate studio, and went to Li's by mistake. Once I smelled the egg rolls, I stayed for lunch."

Steve shook his head in amusement. "How did you happen to be looking for a karate studio?"

"We were working on the radio promotion for a

chain of them and decided to feature the woman's point of view—you know, self-defense and all. I wanted to watch a class so that I would have a better feel for the copywriting."

"Did you ever find the karate studio?"

"After lunch, I did. It was in the next block. Actually, I ended up taking a lesson. It was fun."

"You're one of a kind, Kate," he said, laughing. His expression became thoughtful then. "You really don't stint on your work."

"I like what I do. There's always something new and different to pique my interest."

"But mainly you like the excitement?"

"It isn't all exciting. Like most jobs, it has moments that I find less than enchanting."

"Such as?"

"Too many parties and receptions, making command performances at social events with people I barely know—if I know them at all."

"Then why do you go to these things?"

She shrugged. "Because my boss considers it to be part of my job."

He studied her curiously for a moment then dropped the subject. Glancing across the room at an easel which held a stack of sketches, he asked. "May I take a look at your work?"

"By all means. It's in pretty rough form, of course, but I'd like you to see what I do."

They walked to the easel, where he studied the sketches while Kate explained their concepts to him. He listened intently to her description of the various projects she was working on. When he put down the sketches, his admiration was apparent. "I can see why you get so many assignments. You're a very talented woman, Kate."

"I love this part of my work."

"I can understand why you do. You're very good at it."

"I could happily spend all my time on the artistic part of the job and let other people do the selling and promotion. That's another part of my job I find less than enchanting. And someday, after I've got my training behind me, I hope to be able to limit myself to the part of the work that I enjoy."

He turned away from the easel to study her intently. "I admire you for knowing what you want and having the courage to go after it, and I wish you every success with your career. But I have to say that I also hope there's room in your life for something more."

There was an urgency in his words that drew Kate's eyes to his. "Work isn't everything, Steve. I know that."

"I hope so, because I like being with you." The intensity in his voice matched the appeal in his expression as he took her hands in his. "I want a place in your life, too, Kate," he said.

He bent his head to hers, and Kate's face lifted as though drawn by a magnet. Of their own volition, her lips found his. His kiss was gentle, tender, unbelievably sweet. Time stopped for Kate, and it was Steve who at last drew away. Senses spinning, she lingered within the circle of his arms until, reluctantly, he released her. "Make room for me, Kate," he said softly.

Shaken, Kate went through the next moments like a sleepwalker. She made conversation automatically, barely aware of what she said.

When he left, promising to telephone her the next day, she managed to make intelligent replies. Then she sank down on the sofa, still giddy from his kiss. Her response to it had been unlike anything she had ever before experienced.

Never had she imagined such feelings. Marveling at her reaction, she struggled to untangle her confusing thoughts, to understand Steve's bewildering effect on her. And as she tried to rein in her runaway emotions, an incredible possibility occurred to her. Was this how it felt? she asked herself in wonder. Could it be that she was falling in love?

CHAPTER 6

ALTHOUGH KATE HAD SPENT far less time over the weekend than she had intended on her review of the Jason files, she made up for it on Monday morning. Steve had been right. The day of rest did wonders for her. By the time her co-workers arrived, she had managed to absorb a surprising amount of the data contained in the file.

She was pleased, too, to find that she was beginning to get a feel for the philosophy of the Jason organization. Its various enterprises were innovative, yet soundly conceived. Perhaps the key word to their business approach was "responsible." Definitely, Jason Enterprises was a prudently and skillfully directed concern, and it seemed to Kate that this was the image that should be depicted in its publicity.

She was busily jotting down ideas for possible promotion when she was interrupted by a telephone call. Her spirits soared as she identified the voice on the other end of the line.

"I couldn't wait until tonight to call you. I wanted to tell you how much I enjoyed our day together.

Somehow, I seem to have gotten distracted last night and never got around to telling you," Steve Turner said.

Remembering the circumstances under which he had departed the evening before, Kate's heart beat a little faster. "I enjoyed the day, too," she replied.

"Enough to repeat it next weekend?"

"Definitely."

"Then I'm putting in my bid early for Saturday night and Sunday." He paused. "Maybe I'm pressing my luck, but I did love being with you, Kate."

"I had a wonderful time," Kate said softly.

"Then it's a date for next weekend?" His voice reflected his satisfaction.

"It's a date."

"In that case, I'm going to get off the phone while I'm ahead and let you get back to work. I'll call you tonight, and we'll make plans."

Kate replaced the telephone in its cradle, contemplating it dreamily while she luxuriated in her pleasure at Steve's telephone call. She couldn't think of a nicer way to start a day. Nor a better way to start the week than with the certainty that she would be seeing him again next weekend.

She was happily considering the prospect when an authoritative voice broke into her thoughts. She looked up to see Clint Hansen standing beside her desk. His stormy expression conveyed an unmistakable displeasure.

"I'd like to see you in my office, Kate," he directed. "I think we need to have a talk." Without further words, he strode off. Bewildered, Kate followed along behind him.

In his office, he went immediately to the source of his dissatisfaction. "I'd like an explanation from you," he said frostily, "although I can't think of an acceptable one under the circumstances."

"I don't understand," Kate said, perplexed.

"I'd like to know what you were doing that was important enough to keep you out of pocket all day. I tried until after seven o'clock last night to get in touch with you."

"You must just have missed me. I was at home from about seven-thirty on."

"But it was too late at seven-thirty. I needed you at six."

"I'm sorry, Clint. I had no idea . . ." Kate began.

"That's exactly the point. You *didn't* have any idea. No idea or any thought of what might be required of you," Clint interrupted. "And I must say I'm surprised. You know how important it is that you be available when I need you? How could you just go traipsing off, leaving me no way to get in touch with you? Particularly now, when the Jason account is on the line."

"Has there been some development on the account?" Kate asked eagerly, her attention captured.

Clint cast an impatient glance at her. "Of course not. We haven't even got anything off the ground yet. And, I might add, we're not likely to get anything going if *all* of us are out gathering daisies instead of attending to business."

"I did attend to business—my part of it, at least," Kate defended herself. "I've already started a list of promotion ideas."

"Which will be of little use to us if we never get a chance to present them," Clint retorted sulkily.

"I thought we were already set up to do a presentation for the Jason people."

"But in the meantime it's only good sense to make sure we stay on target with them. It won't do us much good to work on an expensive presentation only to find that our prospective client has got away. A fish isn't caught until you've got him in the boat, Kate."

Kate had to suppress her own irritation. "The Jason people don't strike me as the kind who go back on their word. If they said they would consider a presentation, I believe them."

"And I believe in taking out a little insurance to make certain they don't change their minds. In this business, out of sight means out of mind, and I intend to be very much on their minds while this deal is working. That means remaining highly visible, which is what I was doing last night. And I could have used a little help from you." Clint continued to glare at Kate as he added, "I must say you picked a fine time to do a disappearing act. Where were you, anyhow?"

Kate was reluctant to answer. She was not ready to talk about her outing with Steve, not wanting to spoil the pleasure of it by quarreling over it with Clint. "What was so important about last night?" she asked instead.

"I had a last-minute invitation to the press party announcing the opening of the new supper club at Jason's Parkview Hotel. Naturally their top PR people were there. It was a perfect opportunity for us to make Brownie points with them—except that you weren't there to make them."

Kate could only feel relieved that she had been spared another of the noisy, crowded functions she had come to dread. Usually deteriorating into shouting matches between strangers, they seemed to her pointless affairs to be attended out of courtesy—and as briefly as possible.

"I doubt very much that I was missed in the least," she said to Clint with a skeptical smile. "At a party as large as that one, nobody ever remembers who was there."

Her remark annoyed Clint all the more. "I don't consider that judgment to be yours to make. I'll decide when this agency needs to be represented at a function and who needs to be there to represent it. There were people at the party last night whom I felt we needed to meet, and you were the person I wanted to meet them. I expect help from the employees of this agency when I need it, Kate. I'm only surprised that you have to be reminded of that fact."

Kate was taken aback by the cutting edge to his voice. "Naturally, I would have been there if I had known you considered it that important, Clint. I'm sorry I didn't find out about it soon enough to go."

"That's the point, Kate. There shouldn't have been any possibility that you wouldn't know. You can't just wander off where you can't be reached for hours."

"I didn't expect to be gone so long," Kate tried to explain. "When I left home, I thought I would be back by midafternoon."

"Then why weren't you?"

"I—it just took longer than I expected," Kate said defensively. "And I had no idea I would be needed. After all, it was Sunday."

"It doesn't matter what day it was. In our business, we work whenever we're needed. Our jobs require total commitment, and there's no room at this agency for people who can't give it."

Kate was jolted by Clint's reprimand. Never before had he questioned her commitment to her career. "You know I put my job before everything else," she exclaimed.

He studied her grudgingly for a moment. Then, his anger dissipated, he said with a shrug, "There's nothing to be gained by squabbling over this. I think we both understand where we're coming from. We can better use our time considering future plans." He took a seat on the edge of his desk and, his usual suave manner returning, regarded Kate with a smug smile. "I did manage to accomplish something at the press party last night. We've been invited to the private opening of an art gallery one of the Jason associates is backing. His wife is involved in the venture, and he's giving it his special attention. Needless to say, the opening will be a very posh, select affair—black tie dinner, movie celebrities, the works. It's quite a feather in our cap to be included, so be at your best."

"Do you mean that I'm invited, too?" Kate asked in surprise.

"My invitation includes a guest. Naturally, I want that guest to be you."

"When is the party?"

"Next Saturday evening. You'll have time to pick up something special to wear. And don't worry about upstaging the other ladies. In this crowd, you'll have all you can do to hold your own. Choose something special, Kate, and charge it to the agency. I consider it a necessary cost of doing business."

His ill temper forgotten, he moved on to a discussion of Kate's work assignments for the coming week. He took it for granted that she had agreed to his plan for Saturday night. It was only after she was back at her desk that she permitted herself to consider her unhappy situation. Obviously, she couldn't go to the gallery opening with Clint and keep her date with Steve. Just as obviously, she couldn't refuse Clint's request—at least, not if she wanted a job to come to on Monday morning.

Dolefully, she considered the only option open to her. She had to break her date with Steve.

Kate was late getting home from work that evening. The day had been hurried and tiring, filled with small aggravations. Her humor was not improved by the knowledge that she was going to have to tell Steve their Saturday night date was off.

She knew she shouldn't be so dismayed by the prospect. After all, her work had to come first. She couldn't permit herself to be distracted by thoughts of an attractive doctor, no matter how intriguing he might be. Clint was certainly right about one thing: she had to get herself and her priorities in hand. She couldn't let the promise of an enjoyable evening jeopardize the success she had worked so hard to achieve.

Still, she found herself nervous and uncertain when Steve telephoned shortly after she arrived home. Anxiously, she awaited his reaction as she explained her situation to him.

"I truly don't want to cancel out, Steve, but I haven't any choice. If my boss tells me to go to the gallery opening, I have to go. It's part of my job. I hope you understand."

"Of course I do. As a doctor, I'm used to emergencies that interfere with things I'd like to do. There will surely be times when I'll have to cancel out at the last minute, however much I might regret it."

"I'm glad you don't mind," Kate said, relieved.

"I didn't say I don't mind. I only said I understand. Actually, I don't like the idea at all. I was looking forward to seeing you."

"I was looking forward to Saturday, too," Kate confessed.

"Well, at least we still have Sunday. Surely your boss won't come up with any plans for you then."

One couldn't count on it, Kate told herself wryly, but she didn't admit her concern to Steve. She could certainly count on being free for church and, likely, for lunch. She refused to think beyond that.

The week was rushed but rewarding. Clint's staff meeting concerning the Jason account went well. He was pleased with Kate's ideas, and gave her approval to develop them for presentation to the Jason people later that month. Caught up in her enthusiasm for the project, she barely noticed the days slipping by.

On Saturday night, she dressed dutifully in the dress of amethyst satin she had chosen to wear to the opening of the art gallery. Clint was pleased by her choice. And, though she had considered the event to be simply an unavoidable duty, it turned out to be an enjoyable affair. The gallery was beautifully designed, an impressive collection of artwork on display. The food and entertainment were planned with a discreet elegance that befitted the distinguished guests, among whom were some of the city's most influential citizens.

Kate recognized several members of the Jason public relations staff and soon struck up a conversation with them. One of them, a young woman of Kate's age named Linda Grant, was particularly interesting. As they talked, she and Kate found that they shared many ideas and opinions about their work. Kate was disappointed when Clint interrupted their conversation to claim her attention elsewhere.

"For goodness' sake, Kate, get out and circulate," he prodded her as he grasped her arm and herded her through the crowd. "You didn't get all dressed up to come here and stand in the corner talking to the Jason office help. Everybody who is anybody is here tonight, and you ought to be taking advantage of the opportunity to meet such important people."

"Except that they may not have all that much interest in meeting *me*," Kate said dryly.

Clint shot an annoyed glance at her. "That's their problem. It's up to you to see that you meet them and make a good impression. You never know when contacts like these are going to pay off. I shouldn't have to remind you that in our business contacts are the name of the game."

Clint's words indicated an opportunistic attitude that troubled Kate, an insincerity with which she fervently disagreed. She disliked the thought of using people. There had to be sincerity in business as well as social relationships, and she refused to believe that people were prompted entirely by the prospect of personal gain. For that matter, she did not believe that Clint was as insincere as his words indicated. He simply let himself get carried away by his ambitions at times.

Fortunately, they were joined then by a group of Clint's acquaintances, and he made no further criticism of Kate. At dinner, he was his usual, agreeable self, and the evening passed pleasantly enough.

When the party was over and Clint had taken her home, the evening's events slipped quickly from Kate's mind. As she drifted off to sleep, her thoughts centered on a single subject: tomorrow she would be seeing Steve.

Sunday was everything Kate had hoped for. It was a lovely, sunny day touched with the first chill of fall, a day whose golden autumn beauty begged to be enjoyed. After church, Steve suggested lunch at a quaint Japanese tea room that overlooked a pretty park. They lingered over their meal and then spent a leisurely hour strolling in the park and admiring the vividly colored beds of chrysanthemums that lined the walkways.

"How do you find all these wonderful places?" Kate asked as she sank down on a park bench to relax in the sun. "For a person who is as new in town as you are, you certainly know your way around."

"I have Rose Stanley to thank again. I get all my tips from her."

"She should write a newspaper column on 'Places to go in Dallas.' She's certainly an expert on the subject," Kate remarked.

"Rose is an expert on a lot of subjects. She's indispensable to Dr. Wallace and me."

Recalling the efficiency of the friendly young nurse, Kate had to agree. "Rose is certainly wonderful with patients. She never makes you feel that you're a bother."

"I should hope not. The patients are the only reason for our being there. And speaking of patients, I'm sorry I didn't think to tell you that I'm on call this weekend. I don't expect any problems because I've already made hospital rounds this morning and everyone was doing well. But I will need to call my service from time to time. I hope you'll understand if there should be an emergency."

"Of course I understand. I'd certainly want to be able to get hold of a doctor if I needed one." Kate was reminded then of her own situation. "As a matter of fact, I'm supposed to be where my boss can reach me later on this afternoon if he should happen to need me. I doubt very much that he will, but I was going to suggest that we go back to my apartment just in case."

"That's fine with me. I can leave your number with my answering service, and neither of us will have to worry about being out of pocket."

They returned to Kate's apartment, and Steve checked with his service. Assured that he was not needed, he joined Kate on the small balcony set off from the living room by sliding glass doors. They left the glass doors open so that the telephone could be heard, positioned their chairs to overlook the garden in the center of the complex, and settled back to enjoy the afternoon.

Totally relaxed, now that the small worry about missing a call from Clint no longer nagged her, Kate sighed contentedly. "I'm glad you didn't mind coming back here. It isn't as pretty as the park, but we can at least be outdoors."

"I'm glad you suggested it. This way I can be sure I won't miss a call and still make the most of the day."

"It does feel good to just sit and relax without feeling guilty, doesn't it?"

"Why should we feel guilty as long as we meet our responsibilities? We're entitled to enjoy our free time."

"What little there is of it?" Kate joked.

Steve smiled. "I thought doctors were short of time until I met you; you seem to be on call more than I am. Are all jobs in advertising as demanding as yours?"

"There isn't much room in the advertising business for low-key people, for sure, but not all agencies are as nonstop as ours. Clint, my boss, believes in being on top of all things at all times, which makes for a busy bunch of employees."

"So I've gathered." He hesitated. "The thing you cancelled out for last night, Kate. Was it a usual thing or something important?"

"A little of both," Kate admitted. "We're working on a very important account, which Clint is pretty uptight about. But I'm also supposed to be available to do last-minute things that come up from time to time."

"What kind of things?"

Kate chose her words carefully. "In our business, there are always press parties, community charity benefits, and business receptions where the agency has to be represented. There are also frequent social affairs we need to attend in order to accommodate our clients and, to be honest, make contacts that might lead to new accounts."

"And this is the kind of thing Clint expects you to do?"

"He considers it an indispensable part of the business." Kate shifted in her chair to face Steve squarely as she tried to explain. "You have to understand about Clint. He is admittedly more ambitious than some of the other people in the business, but he has also been amazingly successful. Eight years ago, he and a partner started their own small agency. Within five years, they were successfully competing with most of the local agencies. Two years ago, Clint was able to buy out his partner, and within the last year, his agency has begun to compete seriously with some of the larger agencies. So while I may not always agree with his methods, I can't argue with their results."

"And if you're going to work for Clint's agency, you're obviously going to do it on his terms," Steve finished for her.

She nodded. "As Clint puts it, working for him requires total commitment. He won't accept anything less."

"I think I get the picture." Steve fell silent and looked away, his attention centering on the garden below.

"It isn't as if it's always going to be this way," Kate hurried to add, anxious for him to understand. "Once I've got my years of training behind me, things will be different."

He shrugged. "You don't have to justify your choices, Kate. If you're happy the way things are, that's what counts."

"Nobody is happy with their job all the time," Kate said impatiently. "I said I like my work. That doesn't mean I like all the partying that goes with it. Most of the time, I'd far rather be somewhere else. And just as soon as I get far enough along to have some say-so in the matter, I plan to make some changes in my schedule."

"Do those changes include making a little more time for me?" he asked with a sudden, disarming smile.

Kate's lips curved in answer. "Most definitely."

"I hope so, because I was beginning to feel a little anxious. I would like to see you more often."

His words held a question. "I'm sure we can arrange it," Kate said quickly. Recognizing the intensity in his eyes, she turned away, not ready for him to see how eagerly she responded to him.

He asked no more questions, and they spent the rest of the afternoon lazily. The climax of the day came when Kate, under his close supervision, prepared an omelet for their supper that he pronounced a triumph. She shared it with him proudly, surprised at the satisfaction she found in her achievement.

He made no further mention of her uncertain schedule until the end of the evening. He paused at the door, leaning forward to tilt her face so that he could look into her eyes. "I would ask if I were going to see you next weekend except that I'm not sure I can wait that long. Do you suppose we could squeeze in a dinner date sometime before then?"

Kate smiled happily. "I think it could be managed."

He nodded, satisfied, and bent down to kiss her tenderly, his lips lingering longingly on hers. "Make time for us, Kate," he whispered. "I think we could have something special."

Dreamily, Kate bade him goodnight. Long after he had gone, her thoughts were still in a turmoil. After today, there was no question about her feelings for Steve. As far as she was concerned, there was already something very special between them. She had no idea what to do about it because it was totally unexpected; she hadn't planned for such an occurrence. But planned or not, it had happened. She had fallen unmistakably in love with Steve.

CHAPTER 7

KATE'S ADMISSION TO HERSELF about her feelings for Steve brought with it a changed outlook. The serenity she had found in being with him carried over into her work, bringing an order to her hectic schedule. The church services they had attended together had a revitalizing effect on her, filling her with a new enthusiasm so that she viewed each day with an eager expectancy.

Admittedly, a good bit of the expectancy centered around Steve. They managed a game of tennis after work on Monday evening, treating themselves to a platter of Li's egg rolls afterward. On Tuesday evening, she found herself jogging with him in the park. Her pace was maddeningly slow and the distance embarrassingly short. Still, even though she finished the course walking, she felt a thrill of satisfaction as she listened to his words of encouragement. There was a wonderful challenge in proving herself to him.

And, though she left the office promptly each afternoon, her work somehow got done quite satisfactorily. By arriving at work early when there were no distractions, she was able to accomplish as much as always. A little organization could work wonders, she told herself proudly. After all, there was such a thing as overkill. Steve was right. There was time to enjoy yourself if you just took it. All you had to do was plan properly.

Her harmonious new schedule lasted until Wednesday afternoon when Clint Hansen returned from the business trip that had taken him out of town for the first part of the week. Kate was ready to leave the office for the day when he appeared unexpectedly at her desk.

"Rustle up something for us to drink and join me in my office. I'll fill you in on the happenings," he directed. From his satisfied expression, Kate guessed that his trip had gone well. Her heart sank. She was planning to have dinner with Steve this evening, and Clint's arrival was sure to cause problems. If he was in a jubilant mood, he would be wanting to talk, and the conversation could go on for hours.

She hesitated uneasily. "As a matter of fact, I had an appointment. Of course, if you need me . . ."

He frowned. "I did want to go over some things with you, but I suppose . . ." He paused, then shrugged in resignation. "Go on to your appointment. My news will keep. Business comes first, of course."

"If you're sure," Kate said uncertainly. She felt guilty for letting him think she was going to be working when in fact she was rushing off to be with Steve. Yet if she told him where she was going, her dinner date would surely be cancelled out.

"First things first," he said with a regretful smile. "For that matter, I can use the time to work my way through the pile of papers on my desk. It does stack up when I'm away."

Kate scooped up her briefcase and hurried away before he could change his mind. Although she felt deceitful and disloyal, her desire to see Steve was stronger than her pangs of conscience.

At home, she had time for a relaxing bubble bath while she waited for Steve to call. Wednesday was a busy day for him since it was Dr. Wallace's day off. She smiled and shook her head. What an unlikely team she and Steve made, she thought. A busy doctor with unpredictable hours and a woman whose job demanded attention around the clock. It was a wonder they managed to see each other at all.

It was almost seven before he finally called, his voice filled with regret. "I'm at the hospital, Kate. A little boy with a bad appendix. I've called in a surgeon, but the parents want me to stay with them. So it looks as though I'm going to be here for the rest of the evening. I guess we'll have to take a rain check on that dinner. I hope you'll understand."

"Of course I do. Naturally your patient wants you with him."

"He's a very small and very scared little boy, who needs all the reassurance we can give him." There was an anxious note in Steve's voice that touched Kate's heart. For the first time, she was fully aware of the heavy responsibility he carried, of the concerns that lay behind his confident manner.

"I'm sure he'll feel safer having you there with him," she agreed.

"I hope so. But I'm going to miss being with you. Do you suppose we could try again tomorrow night?"

"It's hard to say," she said doubtfully, remembering Clint. "My boss will likely keep me late. He has been out of town all week, and things have stacked up."

"Why don't I give you a call anyway?"

"I can't promise anything."

"Neither can I, for that matter. Let's just see what happens. But Kate," his tone intensified, "save Saturday for us."

Kate hesitated. Who could say what plans Clint might turn up with? "I'll try," she said finally. "You know I'd like to."

"Then I'll settle for that," he said softly.

He hung up, leaving Kate to turn away from the telephone, disappointed. She had counted on seeing Steve. As hard as it was to put Clint off, she hated the thought of having done it for nothing. But then she scolded herself for her uncharitable thoughts. Steve had even less control over his schedule than she did. He was, after all, a physician with vital demands on him.

Disconsolately, she opened her briefcase, deciding to make the best of the wasted evening by getting a headstart on tomorrow's work. Having been put off once, Clint could be counted on to claim the major portion of her day. If he ran true to form, he could be expected to claim the rest of the week.

For that matter, Clint was accustomed to having all of her time reserved for him, and he wasn't likely to surrender any of it willingly.

As Kate expected, she received an early summons from Clint on the following morning. He was reading from a thick stack of manila folders when she entered his office. Motioning her to the chair beside his desk, he asked distractedly, "How did the business appointment go? I assume it had to do with the Jason account."

"Not exactly. It was a personal matter," Kate hedged.

He looked up in surprise. "It must have been something special to cause you to rush off the way you did."

"Just something I had to do. And I did take it that you hadn't anything of importance to talk to me about."

A glint of displeasure appeared in his eyes. "That

depends on what you call important, Kate. I should have thought a new assignment would come under that heading—but if you aren't interested . . ."

"Of course I am," Kate said quickly. "I just wasn't expecting anything new to come up, what with all of us tied up on the Jason account."

He shook his head. "No, Kate. We make time for the big push to get the Jason account, but business goes on as usual. Never put all your eggs in one basket. If you drop the basket, the eggs get broken and you're left with nothing." He leaned back in his chair and regarded her shrewdly. "I expect to get the Jason account, of course. As a matter of fact, that was the assignment I wanted to talk to you about."

"Has there been some new development?" Kate asked eagerly. "Have they given us the go-ahead?"

"They're much too astute to make such a premature judgment. We won't get a contract without proving ourselves. It will take the best presentation we can come up with to land them. And that's what I want to talk to you about."

He picked up the folder which held Kate's workup on the Jason hotels and thumbed through it. "I like the approach you've taken on the Jason hotels copy," he said, his displeasure at Kate's defection disappearing as his thoughts moved on to more pressing matters. "You have my approval to go ahead and develop the concept. It projects precisely the image we want."

"I hoped to give the impression not only of quality but of dependability," Kate began.

He interrupted her. "You don't have to explain it to me. It speaks for itself. And I think the same concept could be applied to their Mirror Lake Resort development. That was the assignment I had in mind."

Kate's eyes widened. The property Clint spoke of was an impressive one, a large, rural development of homes and townhouses located in a picturesque, wooded area which fronted on a beautiful lake. It was close enough to the city to be convenient but provided the advantages of a country setting. Still in the developmental stages, it offered a wide choice of housing, excellent boating and fishing facilities, a golf course, tennis courts, and an elegantly designed clubhouse for entertainment and fine dining. The undertaking promised to be a highly successful one. To have a part in its development would be a publicist's dream.

Clint smiled at her reaction. "I see that I've got your attention. Would you like to try your hand at working up something on Mirror Lake Resort?"

"Need you even ask?" Kate exclaimed. "I'd love it, of course."

"I rather thought so, and I've set you up to visit the development and put some ideas together. The Jason people are assigning one of their PR people to act as a guide and brief you on the project." He glanced at the memo pad on his desk. "Linda Grant, I believe her name is."

Kate was pleased at the choice, remembering the pert, enthusiastic young woman she had met when she attended the reception at the newly opened art gallery. "I'll get in touch with her this morning and set something up."

"I thought you might drive down on Sunday. We can't spare any of our precious weekday hours."

"I'll see if Linda can make it."

"Don't see *if* she can make it, Kate. See that she *does* make it. You've got to learn to fit people into your schedule instead of letting them fit you into theirs. I needn't remind you that time is money."

Kate ignored his reprimand. Already her mind was absorbed by her new assignment. "I'll set up the trip and get busy finishing up the hotel layouts. By Sunday, I'll be ready to begin on Mirror Lake." Eager to get on with her work, she rose from her chair and started from the room.

He stopped her before she reached the door. "By the way, we'll be seated with some of the Jason people at dinner Saturday night, so you should be able to pick up some information then."

Kate stared at him blankly. "What dinner?"

"The dinner before the Emerald Charity Ball, of course," he exclaimed in irritation. "Where's your head, Kate? That's the opening event of the fall social season. It has been on the calendar for months."

Kate could hardly confess that her head had been filled with thoughts of an intriguing doctor lately. She mumbled an appropriate reply and made a hasty retreat. Back at her desk, she dismally contemplated the complication that Clint had just introduced. She could hardly go to the Emerald Charity Ball and go out with Steve Turner too.

She managed to tuck the matter away at the back of her mind until she arrived home that evening long after eight o'clock. But then, drained by the long, taxing day, she glumly considered the alternatives she faced. Either she risked arousing Clint Hansen's wrath by missing the Emerald Charity Ball, or she cancelled her engagement with Steve.

Fleetingly, she thought how satisfying it would be to attend the ball with Steve, envisioning the handsome figure he would make in a tux. Then she dismissed the thought with a sigh. Even if he should agree to such a possibility, she felt certain that Clint Hansen would not. Although they had never actually discussed the matter, Clint seemed to take it for granted that Kate would be his companion at such affairs.

Until now, she had given their relationship very little thought. She enjoyed the excitement of working with Clint; he was entertaining and fun to be with. She admired his drive and ambition, his talent and imagination. If there were at times differences in their standards, there was also a harmonious friendship. If they didn't always agree on method, they shared the same long-term goals. He was an attractive, dynamic man any woman would enjoy being with. Beyond that, Kate had given their personal friendship no thought. Absorbed in her work, sharing Clint's enthusiasm for their profession, she had given no consideration to any relationship between them beyond that of good friends who enjoyed each other's companionship and a stimulating work relationship.

Now, though, Kate sensed that Clint would resent the inclusion of another man in her life—if only because such an intrusion would interfere with the very convenient working arrangement they had established. Perhaps that was why she had instinctively avoided telling Clint about her friendship with Steve. She had no doubt that he would object to the time she spent with Steve, and would likely try to put a stop to it. Clint demanded total commitment from the partners in any of his associations.

She wasn't ready to subject her still fragile, blossoming relationship with Steve to the force of Clint's disapproval. It was still too new, too tender to be exposed to outside pressures. She was aware that something special was happening to her, and she wanted to hold onto it.

All of which made the choice that confronted her all the more difficult. She was still struggling with her decision when Steve telephoned.

"I've been trying to call you for the last hour to tell you how much I missed seeing you last night. I hope you know how much I regretted having to cancel out," he began in apology.

"I regretted it, too, but I understand that your patients come first," Kate replied. "How did the little boy weather his surgery?"

"Like a little soldier. I'm sure he'll come along nicely."

"Then I'm happy to have given up an evening's pleasure."

"I'm glad you still consider it a pleasure. I was afraid you might decide you couldn't put up with a doctor's uncertain schedule."

"I would be a fine one to object to somebody else's schedule, wouldn't I?"

"Now that you mention it, you do tend to stay out of pocket. What kept you so late this evening? Or do you mind my asking?"

"Of course I don't mind. And I was working, of course. I got a new assignment today that I'm quite excited about."

He chuckled. "Even though more work seems to be the last thing you need, I'm happy for you—since it seems to be what you want. I should have thought, though, that the account you're working on would be about all you could manage."

"This is just more of the same account, but it offers me an opportunity I'm very pleased about."

"Then I'll be eager to hear about it at dinner Saturday night. What would you think about a return visit to Mama Carelli's?"

Kate's heart gave a thud. "That's something I've got to talk to you about, Steve," she began reluctantly. "I've run into a problem about Saturday night. I'm afraid I forgot all about a business engagement that's been on my calendar for months. It's something I can't get out of, as much as I would like to."

There was a long silence on the line before Steve said finally, "Well, I guess if it's something you have to do, that's the way it has to be. But would I be out of line to ask what kind of business engagement would be scheduled months ahead?"

"Of course not," Kate said quickly. "You see, the agency supports as many charitable events as possible, and this Saturday is the night of the Emerald Charity Ball. Since we use these occasions to entertain clients, I have no choice but to go. I just hadn't remembered that this was the weekend of the ball when we talked about going out that night."

"I can understand why you wouldn't want to miss such an occasion. I'm sure the ball is a very glamorous affair." Steve paused, and a trace of irony tinged his voice. "I'm afraid Mama Carelli's doesn't offer much competition."

"It isn't that, Steve!" Kate exclaimed. "As far as I'm concerned, the ball is just more business entertaining. I don't care much about those crowded affairs, as a matter of fact. It's just that such things are a part of my job." As Kate spoke, it suddenly became very important to her that she make her feelings clear to Steve. "I'd far rather spend the evening at Mama Carelli's with you. I hope you understand that."

"When you put it that way, it helps." His tone brightened. "And we still have Sunday. Maybe we can go to Mama Carelli's then."

Kate's spirits sank. She hadn't the heart to relay the news that she would be tied up on Sunday too. Instead, grasping at possibilities, she suggested hastily, "What about tomorrow night? Are you free then?"

"Patients willing, I plan to be. Shall we try it?"

Kate didn't let herself think of any plans Clint might have made for her. If necessary, she would plead illness, amnesia, insolvency, whatever it took. She had to see Steve and explain to him about the weekend. Otherwise, she would never be able to make him understand. "I'd love it," she asserted valiantly, flouting fate and career. "What time shall I be ready?"

"Knowing your schedule, let's try for eight o'clock—and hope all my patients remain healthy and your clients otherwise occupied."

"It's a date," Kate pronounced.

And it *was* a date, Kate promised herself defiantly

as she replaced the telephone in its cradle. Nothing was going to interfere with her evening out with Steve. Not even if she had to spend it with him at the hospital. Clint could take the rest of her weekend, but tomorrow night belonged to Steve. She had a right to spend some time with him, and she was going to take it.

CHAPTER 8

MAMA CARELLI'S WAS AS WARM and inviting as Kate remembered it, the spicy smell of the food as appetizing, the sound of the soft Italian music as romantic. There was a festive air about the evening as she sat across the candlelit table from Steve. Wearing a cream-colored pullover sweater that accented his blond hair and golden brown eyes, he was even more appealing than she remembered him. As always, his lighthearted amiability brightened her mood.

Sharing the happenings of their separate days, they found an endless number of subjects to talk about. Steve had anecdotes to tell concerning events at his office or the hospital. In turn, Kate sought out his reaction to a promotional packet she was working on. One topic led into another so that hours seemed like minutes as time sped past.

Their dinner was another of Mama Carelli's triumphs. Thin, delicately seasoned veal was accompanied by a delicious eggplant parmigiana, crusty bread, and a flavorful salad. Their dessert of spumoni ice cream was a fitting finale to a delicious meal. They dawdled over after-dinner coffee and then took a walk through the shopping center in which the restaurant was located, window shopping as they strolled. The chill of fall sharpened the crisp night air, and it was exhilarating to be outdoors.

In the pleasure of Steve's companionship, Kate forgot about the complications of the weekend. Nor did Steve mention the plans that had gone awry. They were strolling through the grounds on their way to Kate's apartment when he turned to her questioningly. "Do you think you could manage the early service at church on Sunday? If so, there's an interesting place I'd like to take you to for lunch. It's a good hour's drive from the city, though, and I'm told it starts getting crowded around noon."

Kate hesitated, searching for the best way to explain her predicament and fearing Steve's reaction to it. When she did not answer, he cast a quizzical glance at her. "Or maybe I should first ask if you want to go to church with me on Sunday. Maybe I'm assuming too much."

"Not at all," Kate said hastily. "I love going to church with you. It's just . . ." She took a deep breath and plunged into her explanation. "You see, I have to work on Sunday. It has to do with the account I've been telling you about. I have an appointment to visit one of the client's real estate developments."

"On Sunday morning?" There was an edge of exasperation to Steve's voice.

"The property is a resort development at a lake nearly a hundred miles from here. It will take us a couple of hours to get there."

"Us? I suppose that means you and Clint Hansen."

"Not at all. I'm going with one of the client's PR people. A woman. Her name is Linda Grant."

"I see."

But it was clear to Kate that Steve did not see. The pleasantry of the evening was gone, and a heavy curtain of misunderstanding had dropped between them. "It isn't something I want to do," Kate tried to explain.

"You don't owe me any explanations, Kate."

"I want to explain, though. I want you to understand."

He did not reply, and they walked in silence to the door of Kate's apartment. She made no move to take her door key from her handbag, wanting to prolong their parting, unwilling for him to leave while tension lay between them. "It isn't as if this is a usual thing, Steve. It's just that we have to make every weekday minute count while we're working up the presentation for this account. Everyone is doing double duty now, but once we get the account things will settle down."

"Will they, Kate? It seems to me your schedule has been like this ever since I've known you." There was a skepticism in his tone. In the moonlight, his face was troubled. He seemed to be struggling with his thoughts. "What I wonder," he said at last, "is whether things will ever settle down for you and me."

"They will, Steve. If you can just be patient, I'm sure I can manage things better. Until now, I've never had anything to consider except my job, so I've given it all my time. It will just take a little while for me to rearrange things."

"It isn't only your job, Kate. It's mine, too. A doctor, particularly one just starting out in practice, hasn't any claim on his time. I'm on call constantly. That's why Dr. Wallace brought me into practice with him. His health won't stand the strain any longer, and he needs a younger doctor to be on call nights and weekends. I have only one free weekend a month. So what happens if my free weekend happens to come along when you're tied up? Or if you manage a night free and I have to cancel out at the last minute?"

"I guess we just keep trying to work things out," Kate said.

"Can we, Kate?" There was a note of uncertainty in his voice, a wistfulness in his expression. "Can we make time in our lives for each other?"

"We can if we want to," Kate said softly.

He reached out to caress her cheek ever so lightly with the back of his hand. "I guess that's what I'm really asking. Do you want to, Kate? Do you want to enough to make things work out for us?"

Looking up at his face, so appealingly silhouetted in the moonlight, Kate felt a rush of anxiety. The thought of not being with Steve again brought with it a tremor of dismay. "Oh, yes, Steve, I do want to," she said fervently. "I want to very much."

A sudden intensity flared in his eyes. His arms closed around her, drawing her to him. As his head bent to hers, her lips went eagerly to his. His kiss was searching, questioning, and her heart opened to it in answer. A longing stole over her, a need to share her feelings with him, to express emotions she did not try to analyze.

"That's all I wanted to know, Kate," he whispered, holding her close to him. "If we want to be together, we'll find a way. If you want it as much as I do, somehow we can make it happen."

Kate's arms slipped around his neck, and her cheek settled into the hollow of his shoulder. Secure in his embrace, listening to the vibrant pounding of his heart, she marveled at her emotions. Something special and glorious was happening to her, something wonderful. And she didn't intend to let it slip away. She would find a way for them to be together.

On Sunday morning, Kate dressed for her trip to Mirror Lake with disappointment. A whole, lovely day to be with Steve was lost. Not to mention the church service, which always seemed to brighten her whole week. *It wasn't fair,* she thought mutinously. Clint hadn't the right to ask it of her.

With a sigh, she gathered up her handbag and

briefcase. The sooner she got started, the quicker the job would be done. With luck, she might even be home in time to see Steve that evening, if only for a little while.

In minutes, she was driving down a parkway bordered by the towering office complexes that had mushroomed on the north side of the city, extending the North Dallas "Golden Corridor" for miles. Linda Grant's apartment was located in the area, and Kate found it without difficulty. Linda stepped outside just as Kate parked in front of her apartment door.

Linda made a cheery companion. With a pixie face, lively brown eyes, and a ready smile, she was fun to be with. They struck up a lively conversation, and soon put the city skyline behind them. It was a lovely day, warm and sunny; snowy clouds drifted lazily across a clear, blue sky. The lightly wooded countryside was splashed with scarlet and gold, announcing the arrival of autumn. The highway that cut through the vast expanse of farm and ranch land beckoned invitingly, lending an air of expectancy to their journey.

During their drive, Linda explained the developers' plans for the project. By the time they turned off the highway onto the side road that wound through the development, Kate had a clear understanding of its concept. It was admittedly a bold and costly venture. But as they drove past the attractive homesites and lodges nestled around the mirror-clear lake, her enthusiasm for the project soared. Mirror Lake Resort was a fairyland. Promoting it would be a delight.

They made a thorough tour of the development, taking time off for lunch at the elegantly designed clubhouse that fronted on the lake. The decor of the dining room made their luncheon a special event. Fresh flowers in crystal vases centered tables spread with white linen cloths and set with attractive china and sparkling silver. Soft lighting and lush greenery enhanced the setting.

The food was as appetizing in taste as it was in appearance. Relishing the last of her chicken and green grape salad, Kate observed her surroundings with admiration and remarked to Linda, "I must say that the Jason people have gone all out with this project. The facilities here are fabulous."

"They wanted it to offer the same quality people are accustomed to seeing in their hotels. That makes Mirror Lake an expensive undertaking, of course, but they didn't want to offer the public any less."

"This certainly lives up to the Jason reputation," Kate observed.

"You'll find the same quality in the construction of the homes and lodges. After lunch we'll go through the furnished models so that you can see for yourself." Linda's expression became intent and businesslike as she warmed to her subject. "Incidentally, 'quality' is a good word to keep in mind when you're working on anything for Jason Enterprises. They don't like cutting corners. They're willing to invest what it takes to develop a first-rate project, and they expect to spend what it costs to promote it. But they also expect to get top value for their dollars and will require a superior job. I'm sure you know they aren't noted for being an easy client to satisfy," she added with a smile.

"The best clients never are." Kate regarded Linda curiously. "It must be challenging to work for Jason Enterprises. They seem to have a topnotch staff. I should think it would be very stimulating to work with that caliber of people."

"It is. The management expects the best from its employees, but they offer a great deal in return. We have a maximum amount of freedom in how we do our jobs as long as we get the desired results."

"It was explained to me that any general advertising Jason Enterprises contracts for has to be approved by their public relations department, but I've never understood exactly how the PR department is set up. Exactly what is your job, Linda?"

"There is a PR division that supervises all the advertising and publicity for Jason Enterprises. The general advertising is handled through outside agencies, but the publicity for the various individual operations is handled within the PR department. I'm assigned to the Parkview Hotel. It's my job to publicize the events at the hotel, the entertainers who perform there, the trade shows, any special events or notable guests. And while I report to the PR vice president, I'm allowed to do my work pretty much on my own. I get a good budget to work with and no one bugs me about how I do my job as long as I do it with good taste and project the image established for Jason hotels."

"It must be nice to have such a free hand in your work," Kate said with a trace of envy.

"I couldn't work any other way. I want to be sure I have control of all the details. I don't see how you advertising people skip from one client to another the way you do—and still manage to please them."

"That part doesn't bother me. In fact, I enjoy researching a project and trying to come up with what the client needs. If I could just do the project development and leave all the rest to somebody else, I'd be happy."

"Isn't that pretty much what you do at the Hansen Agency?" Linda asked, seeming a bit surprised. "I got the impression that you were the lead idea person at the agency."

"Thanks, but I'm only one of the hired help."

"But you're always with Clint Hansen wherever the agency is represented."

"That's because Clint thinks the staff should be involved in everything the agency does."

Linda cast a quizzical glance at Kate. "Somehow I got the idea that maybe you and Clint were an item."

"We're good friends, but that hasn't got anything to do with my work assignments," Kate said a bit defensively. "Clint would never let personal considerations influence his business judgment."

Linda held up a silencing hand. "I wasn't suggesting that you weren't in every way qualified to do your job. In fact, you strike me as a very talented woman with a good head for the economics of the business. But they'll never stake you out in a field to scare the crows away from the corn, and Clint is obviously well aware of that. I notice he never lets you stray too far from his side."

"That's just because he wants to be sure I do my job."

"I doubt that. I think he knows a good thing when he sees it—and not just in business. And I must say that as good-looking as he is, most women would consider him quite a catch. Clint Hansen is one very sharp guy."

"I admire Clint tremendously, of course," Kate said quickly. "But we're both too busy with our work to think of personal matters."

Linda laughed. "Nobody is that busy. If I worked every day with a guy as good-looking as Clint Hansen, I'd certainly find time to score some points with him. Unless . . ." She studied Kate speculatively. "Maybe there's someone else?"

The suggestion took Kate quite by surprise, and she hesitated in framing an answer. Linda's lip curved into a broad smile. "So there is somebody else."

"Well, there is this doctor . . ."

Linda's eyes turned heavenward. "One woman should be so lucky. Clint Hansen and a handsome doctor, too."

"I didn't say he was handsome," Kate hedged.

"He's bound to be if he can outshine Clint."

"He's very different from Clint," Kate began and then paused, feeling self-conscious talking about Steve.

Linda seemed to sense her reservation. "It's okay, Kate. Anything you tell me will be held in the strictest confidence. After all, we women have to stick together."

Kate felt herself drawn strongly to Linda, knowing instinctively that here was a woman who could be a true friend, someone she could trust. "I guess the real problem is finding time for a relationship with any man. How do you manage it, Linda? How do you find time for any personal life at all?"

"For the right man, you *make* time," Linda pronounced. "Believe me, I love my job and the excitement of having a place in the business world; but when the right man comes along, I intend to make room in my life for him. A man's career doesn't keep him from having a happy home life and family. Why should a woman's?"

"It's different with women. Or maybe it's the high-pressure business we're in. I never have a free moment from my job."

"Then maybe you need to take a look at your job. Maybe you've bitten off a bigger chunk of career than you can handle. I'll be honest and say I could never work the way you do. Why don't you consider specializing? Limit yourself to the part of the work you like and do best. That's what I've done at Jason Enterprises."

Kate sighed. "If only I could. But Clint doesn't see it that way. He believes in total involvement."

"Total involvement is one thing; spreading yourself too thin is another," Linda said doubtfully.

"I wish I could convince Clint of that. There seems to be a very fine line between the two of them," Kate said ruefully.

"And who am I to question Clint Hansen's methods? His agency's results are dynamite," Linda said with a shrug. "I know one thing, though," she added firmly. "There's more to life than a career. No matter how successful you might be, a career isn't enough if you don't have someone to share it with. If I ever find a man I really love, I'm not going to let him get away."

The conversation moved on then to the day's business, and the two spent a pleasant afternoon completing their tour of Mirror Lake Resort. When they began their return trip home, Kate had a thorough grasp of the project and was ready to begin work on an advertising plan.

It was after eight o'clock by the time she dropped Linda off at her apartment and arrived home. Although she was anxious to talk to Steve, she decided to take time, while her impressions of Mirror Lake Resort were still fresh on her mind, to jot down the ideas that had occurred to her concerning its promotion. Clint would be expecting a report first thing in the morning, and she wanted to be ready for his questions. Also, she wanted to save her conversation with Steve until she could relax and enjoy it.

She had almost finished the memo when the telephone rang. She hurried to answer, expecting the call to be from Steve. Instead, the call was from Clint. He seemed pleased that her trip had gone well but did not press her for details. "They'll keep until tomorrow when we've got more time," he said. "I'm at dinner with some people, but I managed to duck out long enough to call you. Incidentally, I've been busy today, too. I think you'll be pleased to hear what I've been up to. I'll tell you all about it tomorrow."

He hung up hurriedly, leaving Kate curious but unconcerned. She was used to Clint's surprises. One never knew what he was going to do next, and she had long ago learned not to try to guess. He would let her know what he had on his mind in his own time and in his own way.

She returned to the memo she had been working on. It was after nine o'clock by the time she finished it.

Tired but satisfied, she put in a call to Steve, ready to reward her dedication to duty with a pleasant, leisurely chat with him.

Her telephone call to him, though, was taken by his answering service. Steve was at the hospital attending a patient and couldn't be reached at present nor likely for the rest of the evening. Kate turned away from the phone in disappointment. The day seemed incomplete. She had counted on being able to talk to him for a little while.

Disheartened, she got ready for bed only to find herself mulling over her conversation at lunch with Linda Grant, finding in it an irony. Linda could talk all she liked about accommodating personal lives and careers, but it was much easier to talk about than to do. Particularly if you worked for as ambitious a man as Clint and were trying to adjust your schedule to accommodate a busy doctor.

Dejectedly, Kate regarded the silent telephone, wishing that there was some way she could get in touch with Steve. She sorely needed to share her thoughts with him, to be reassured by him, to talk to him. Because, however much they might say they wanted it, however wonderful it might be, they were never going to manage any kind of relationship if it was going to be this hard for them to be together. Somehow they were going to have to find a way to make time for one another.

CHAPTER 9

As KATE EXPECTED, SHE received an early summons from Clint the following morning. She found him in the best of spirits. Greeting her enthusiastically, he seated her on the sofa, indicating that this was to be an informal chat. This impression was reinforced when he served her coffee in one of the china cups and saucers from a coffee service on a low table beside the sofa. Clint insisted that visitors to his office be served with china and silver, deeming styrofoam cups to be an affront.

Kate wondered what she had done to deserve such attentiveness—or, more likely, what she was going to be asked to do. But she left it to him to direct the conversation.

"I was pleased to hear that your trip to Mirror Lake turned out so well. From our conversation last night, I gathered you got what you were looking for."

"I think I got a very good feel for what the Jason people are trying to do and the impression they want to give in their advertising. I have several ideas we might pursue if you have time to talk about them."

"Use your own judgment, Kate. I'm sure you'll hit on the best approach. When you get something put together, I'll take a look at it; but for now, I'm sure you can do very well on your own."

"Thanks for the vote of confidence," Kate said guardedly. It wasn't like Clint to be this effusive in his praise.

"You've earned it by your performance," he said, regarding her approvingly. "You're doing a fine job. Your work on the Jason account is shaping up very well."

"Let's hope the Jason people think so when they see our presentation."

"We'll make sure they do." Clint's voice held a confident ring, but his face took on a determined expression. "Whatever it takes, this agency is going to deliver it. We're not going to blow this chance."

"We'll give it our best shot," Kate assured him.

"I'm sure you will. Everybody who is assigned to this account knows how important it is to the agency. I know you're all willing to do however much work it may take to land it." The firm set of his jaw relaxed then, and he bestowed a benign smile upon Kate. "And speaking of work, I got so busy Friday evening that you ducked out of the office before I could catch you. I called you later, but you were out and about somewhere. I meant to mention it Saturday night but never got the chance to be alone with you."

"You were playing host to a sizable group of guests," Kate said, trying to turn the subject away from her defection on Friday evening. She had purposely slipped away so that Clint could not tie her up and interfere with her dinner date with Steve.

Clint was not to be distracted, however. "Where were you Friday night, anyhow?"

"There was just something I had to do." Kate reached for the coffee carafe as a diversionary tactic and offered to refill Clint's cup.

An amused smile played at the corners of his mouth as he watched her pour the coffee. "You know, Kate, I might think you were keeping secrets from me except that we both know that sort of thing isn't necessary between us. We've been together too long. How long is it now? Three years?"

"Just about."

"And three good ones, too. We hit it off well, Kate. We make a good team. And even if I don't show it—for that matter, it would cause problems for you with the rest of the staff if I did—you and I both know that you're special. You've got the same drive I have, the same desire to succeed. We're going to do big things together, you and I." His voice softened, and he leveled a discerning glance at her. "We've got a great thing going for us, Kate, and I'm sure neither of us is going to let anything—or anybody—spoil it for us."

Not knowing how to interpret his words, Kate did not reply. If he noticed her hesitancy, he did not show it. Setting his cup down, he moved to another subject. "To show you what kind of guy I am, I've been busy in our behalf over the weekend. As I told you last night, you're going to be pleased when you hear what I've done." He leaned back to observe her expectantly. "I've arranged for us to spend next weekend at Jason's very posh new Conference Center in Houston."

Kate tried not to show her dismay at his announcement. The last thing she wanted was to be tied up on another weekend. Clint seemed not to notice her reaction, however, as he enthusiastically outlined his plans. "Of course, it'll be a working weekend, but we'll take time for some relaxation, too. As you undoubtedly know, this Conference Center is something special."

The center Clint referred to was the most recent Jason venture. It was designed to accommodate business conferences, offering complete hotel services, meeting rooms, auditorium space, and recreational facilities. It followed the newest concepts in conference accommodations and was considered to be an innovation.

"I plan for all the staff members assigned to the Jason presentation to make the trip," Clint continued. "You can take a look at the Jason hotel; Sally Hines will have an opportunity to do a final inspection of the shopping mall Jason invests in; Seth Barrow can check out any remaining questions about their computer holdings. Doug Siegel is making the arrangements, since he has already visited the center in working on his coverage of Jason's commercial real estate. My contribution was to wrangle the invitation from Jason's PR vice president," he added with a pridefully arched brow.

Kate's interest stirred. "I've heard about the center, of course. Doug says it's fabulous."

"A really innovative concept. It provides every service that could possibly be required for a successful business conference, including relaxing the minds and bodies of the participants. I thought we could go to Houston on Friday and use the day to do any fact-finding we still need. On Saturday we can start putting together a preliminary presentation. With all of us working together without interruptions or outside distractions, we should come out of the weekend with a pretty good idea of where we stand. And, if we don't run into any snags, we ought to be able to find a few minutes to relax a bit while we're tending to business."

It was exhilarating to think about being this close to finalizing all the work they had done on the Jason account. Kate's pulses quickened at the prospect. Seeing ideas take tangible form was the part of her work she liked best. It was at this stage that it all came together. In a medium of ideas, it was a moment of realization, the time when you either failed or succeeded. Kate listened absently as Clint finished outlining his plans and then hurried back to her desk. All other considerations were forgotten as her thoughts centered on the work she had to do to be ready for the weekend meeting.

Kate arrived home late that evening, carrying a bulging briefcase. Changing into jeans and a pullover, she made herself a quick pimiento cheese sandwich, brewed a pot of tea, and settled in for an evening of work.

She had barely finished the sandwich when the telephone summoned. The call was from Steve. "You're hard to get hold of. I called you a couple of times earlier to see if you wanted to go jogging but got no answer. What have you been up to that kept you working so late? I should have thought that, having spent a full day at it yesterday, you would have been pretty well caught up."

"We're moving into the final stages of the Jason project. Things get a little tense about this time."

"I can imagine. But at least it's good to hear you speaking in terms of final stages. Does that mean that maybe you're going to have a little more free time soon?" His tone was a bit wistful as he added, "I missed you yesterday."

"I missed you, too," Kate confessed. "I called you when I got back in town, but you were at the hospital."

"I didn't get home until after midnight. I was with a coronary patient. It was touch-and-go for awhile."

"I hope everything went well," Kate said with concern.

"He's going to make it, I think. But he got a good scare—we all did—so maybe he will be persuaded to alter his lifestyle for the better. And speaking of lifestyles . . . ," he began.

"Don't lecture," Kate warned, anticipating his train of thought.

He laughed. "I wouldn't think of it. I was only going to ask if you had a pleasant day at Mirror Lake."

"I accomplished what I needed to, and Linda was fun to be with. But I missed church services—and I missed being with you," she added softly.

"That makes me feel better. I spent a pretty lonely day without you yesterday. I don't suppose, as late as it is, that there's any chance of seeing you tonight."

Kate was torn between duty and desire. The thought of being with Steve was tempting. Yet she had to finish the work she had brought home, and she knew she would accomplish nothing once she had seen him. He seemed to have an utterly disrupting effect upon her. There was also the problem, too, she thought guiltily, of telling him about the coming weekend trip. She felt sure he wasn't going to be happy about it, and she didn't want to risk a misunderstanding with him. She would need time to make him understand.

"Why don't I get caught up on my work tonight, and maybe we can have dinner tomorrow night," she suggested. "In fact, if you're feeling really brave, I'll make dinner for us here. I guarantee that it will be edible."

"Edible or not, I accept. As a man of courage, I'm willing to take the risk."

Kate didn't confide that the real risk would be whether there was any dinner at all. As busy as Clint was with his preparations for the weekend work session, it was unlikely that he would have need of her. But where Clint was concerned, predictions could never be made with any certainty. She could only hope for the best and take her chances. At least, tomorrow was Steve's night off so that there shouldn't be any complications from his schedule.

"I'll make you eat those words—no pun intended," she told Steve.

"I'll eat whatever I can get without complaint," he countered.

They made arrangements for the following evening, and Kate returned to her work with buoyed enthusiasm. As always, talking to Steve had a way of brightening her spirits and inspiring optimism. It would work out tomorrow night, she told herself with confidence. And she had a right to some time with Steve if she was going to give up another weekend. She would also have a much better chance of making him understand about her coming trip to Houston.

The following day went smoothly, and Kate was able to get home in time to prepare a respectable meal. By the time Steve was due to arrive, she had put the chicken in the oven to bake and made a salad of peach halves and cottage cheese. Broccoli spears were simmering, and a quick-mix rice dish was ready to cook; frozen strawberries were thawing to be served over the angel food cake she had bought at the bakery. No gourmet meal, to be sure, but one she needn't be ashamed of. The great American supermarket, friend of the working woman, never ought to be underestimated, she thought with satisfaction.

She had also managed to freshen her makeup and change into comfortable pants and a becoming pullover sweater. She glanced with approval at the dining table that was set with blue placemats and candles and festively centered by the pink carnations she had picked up at the supermarket. *Very nicely done, Kate,* she told herself as she hurried to the door in answer to Steve's knock.

She was unbelievably happy to see him. They both began talking at once, each eager to share with the other the day's events. Somehow when they were together there was so much to talk about, so many questions to be answered, so many things to laugh about.

To Kate's pleasure, Steve pronounced the dinner a triumph. "You can cook for me every night, if you like," he said as he finished his cake.

"Except that I would soon run out of menus. I'm afraid the list is somewhat limited."

"Who needs variety? Being with you is quite suspenseful enough."

"I'm not sure I know how to take that," Kate objected.

"As a compliment. The suspense is in wondering if I'll get to be with you at all."

"Well, at least we don't get bored with one another," Kate joked.

"There could never be a dull moment with you," he replied with a grin. "There never are enough of them."

"I'm going to end this discussion while I'm still ahead. Besides, I have something to tell you," Kate said, pushing back her chair. Refusing Steve's help with the dishes, she ushered him into the living room, and they settled down on the sofa companionably.

"This news of yours, is it good or bad?" Steve looked at her questioningly.

"Well, it's good news and bad news," Kate said. "Which do you want first?"

"The good news."

"Well, then, we're ready to finalize the presentation we've been working on. If Clint approves it, we'll be ready to show it to our prospective client."

"That is good news," Steve said, genuinely pleased. "I suppose the bad news is waiting to see if the client accepts it."

"Not exactly." Kate paused, framing her words carefully. "I'm going to Houston with the other staff members next weekend to do the final work on the presentation."

His smile faded. "Why Houston?"

"Because the Jason Conference Center is there—

as well as some other properties we need to check out. At the Conference Center, we'll have all the facilities we need and can work without distraction. Mainly, though," she added hastily as she noted his guarded expression, "the Center, as the newest of Jason's ventures, is an important part of our promotional package, and Clint thinks we all ought to see it. He says it's a fabulous place."

"I'm sure it is."

There was a marked lack of enthusiasm in his voice, and Kate moved hurriedly to counteract it. "The best thing, of course, is that we'll be winding up the project. All of us are ready to get back to our normal routines."

"Even Clint?"

Although his tone was mild, Kate noticed a tight little line at the corner of his mouth. "Clint will have to slow down for awhile if we get this account. Added to the accounts we already have, the agency will have about all the work it can handle. Unless he wants to hire and train some new people, of course. And in the meantime, the rest of us ought to get a little breather."

"From some of the social events, too?"

Kate did not miss the irony in his question. "I would hope so," she said uneasily. "Clint ought to be pretty well occupied—at least for awhile."

Steve pushed his coffee cup away with an impatient gesture. "You know, Kate, you ought to have something to say about how you spend your free time—assuming Clint considers you to have any."

"That's the trouble," Kate tried to explain. "Up to now, I've pretty much given all my time to my job. It's just going to take Clint a little while to get used to the idea that I expect some time for myself. Getting the Jason account would certainly help things along. Since we'll be too busy to take on any more clients, there shouldn't be the need for many social events."

Steve studied her silently for a moment. "What happens if you don't get the Jason account, Kate?" he asked at last. "Do things just go on as they have been?"

Kate hesitated, not wanting to deal with the possibility. "I guess it'll just take a little longer to work things out," she said finally. Then, thrusting aside the uncomfortable thought, she held her hand out to Steve in a conciliatory gesture and said lightly, "One way or another, things are going to work out. And in the meantime, I intend to think positively. Whatever happens, some of the pressure will come off. We'll be busy, of course, but it should be a more relaxed situation."

An unreadable expression dropped over Steve's face, and he did not seem to notice her outstretched hand. "Then I hope things go well for you this weekend, and I wish you the best of luck with your presentation."

Kate was puzzled by his reaction. She was relieved that he accepted her absence this weekend but disappointed that he showed no pleasure at her announcement that she soon would be less involved in her work. "Once this is behind us, I expect to have a lot more free time," she said, watching him closely.

"That would be a definite improvement." But his tone was undemonstrative, his expression noncommittal.

Baffled by his response, she asked, "You do understand about this weekend?"

"Of course. Your work has to come first. That's understandable."

"Then you don't mind?" Kate pressed him.

"Whether I mind or not has nothing to do with it, Kate. You have to do what you think you ought to do."

Kate changed the subject to a light, amusing one, and he responded dutifully, but there was a curious detachment in his attitude. A barrier seemed to have dropped between them. At a loss to know how to deal with it, Kate tried valiantly to rescue the evening. But, though Steve was pleasant and attentive, she could not recapture their earlier companionable relationship.

He left early, thanking her for the dinner. At the door, he said politely, "I hope it goes well this weekend. I'll try to get in touch with you before you leave town."

"It would help to know you're on my side," Kate said, sorely needing his approval.

"Of course I want you to succeed, Kate. I know how important it is to you." He patted her shoulder lightly. "Go along on your trip, and put your mind on your work. I'll be wishing you the best."

After he had gone, Kate dejectedly cleared the dining room table, feeling disappointed and disheartened that her optimistic efforts had been in vain. The burned-down candles no longer looked festive. The carnations seemed to droop in their crystal vase. The evening she had planned so hopefully had failed. In spite of Steve's pleasant manner and courageous words, she knew he had not understood at all. Her job had finally come between them. She knew it with a certainty because he had left without kissing her goodnight.

CHAPTER 10

IT WAS LATE SUNDAY NIGHT when Kate returned from Houston, tired but satisfied. The Hansen staff members had accomplished their mission. Their work on the Jason project was complete.

Clint had planned the weekend so that they could make the most of every minute. They had flown to Houston and back on a chartered plane. A limousine was waiting to transport them from the airport. There had been only one flaw in his plans, Kate thought as she tumbled wearily into bed. They had arrived home too late for her to telephone Steve.

Nor was she any more successful in reaching him on Monday. She had barely begun to sort out her day when Clint called a luncheon meeting, at which he announced that their presentation to the Jason people was scheduled for Friday. In the flurry of excitement over his announcement, the hours rushed past like minutes as the staff made final preparations for the important event.

Busy as she was, however, Kate noticed that Steve made no effort to contact her. When, by Tuesday evening, he still had not telephoned, she decided it was time for her to take matters in hand. This was his night off, and she might find him at home.

She waited until well after six to call and was pleased when he answered the phone. "It's Kate," she said. "How did the weekend go?"

"It passed." Steve's tone was strangely noncommittal. "How was your trip?"

"It was a good one. We accomplished what we set out to do. We're scheduled to do our presentation this Friday, so we'll be finished with the project by the end of the week. For the present, at least," she added quickly. "Naturally, we're hoping our proposal will be accepted."

"I hope it works out for you. I know what a disappointment it will be to all of you if it isn't accepted."

"Let's don't even think about it," Kate said with a little shiver.

"We'll definitely think positively," Steve agreed.

A silence fell between them as Steve initiated no further conversation. After a moment, Kate said, a bit awkwardly, "How was church Sunday? I suppose you went."

"I did, and the services were enjoyable, as always. Or at least they are to me."

"To me, too, Steve," Kate said, sensing an inference in his words that she wanted to dispel. "I missed being at church." Somehow she didn't feel comfortable in adding that she had also missed being with him.

"There'll be other Sundays. And I'm glad your weekend went well. I'm sure you're pleased to be finishing up your project after working so hard on it. I'll be interested in knowing how your presentation goes."

"I'll be in touch," Kate said, lacking anything further to say. She wanted to continue the conversation but, when Steve did not pursue it, felt she had no choice but to end it. She turned away from the telephone, hurt that Steve had not suggested coming over—which was probably just as well since she had to work anyhow. But at least he could have asked.

For that matter, he hadn't seemed as glad to hear from her as she had expected. In fact, the more she thought about their brief and unsatisfactory conversation, the more disturbed about it she became. Steve had not only failed to suggest seeing her this evening; he had said nothing at all about seeing her during the coming weekend.

On Friday, Kate approached the presentation to the Jason people nervously, but with confidence. When it was time for her to present the promotional packet she had worked up, she was eager to express the thoughts that had developed in her mind over the past weeks.

"My focus," she said, ending her presentation, "is to convey to the public my impressions of Jason Enterprises. As I've studied the Jason operations, one word has continued to occur. That word is integrity, now synonymous in my mind with the Jason name. This is the image I'm promoting. The Jason name on an operation means the consumer can count on getting the promised excellent quality and dependability of service."

After the meeting was over, Kate was oddly calm and relaxed. Whether or not the client accepted the Hansen Agency's promotional package, she was satisfied with her part in it. She had captured the image of the client as she perceived it and put it in tangible form. She had succeeded in doing what she had set out to do.

Clint called the team together to compliment them. "You've done a fine piece of work, and you should be proud," he told them. "If the agency doesn't land this contract, then it is Jason Enterprises who will be the loser." But after the others had gone, he confided to Kate in jubilation, "We've done it, Kate. We've got ourselves a contract. I could feel it when I talked to the Jason people before they left."

"I thought the presentation went very well, but it seems like tempting fate to take anything for granted," Kate said cautiously.

"I know. But I've got a feeling about this. I think we're going to land this contract. I could tell they really liked what we did." He gave her a hug. "You know, of course, that your part of the package was what gave it that little extra zip. You did a fantastic job. You came up with the perfect image for the client. If we get this contract, a lot of the credit will go to you."

"I won't care who gets the credit if we get the account," Kate said.

"Loyally spoken but shortsighted. With an account the size of Jason Enterprises, we'll have to take on some more personnel. And that means some promotions within the agency." Clint grinned at her knowingly. "Do you think you could cope with an executive position?"

"I expect I could live with it," Kate said, smiling in return.

He gave her another enthusiastic hug. "That's my Kate. And, for the record, there will be a reward in this for you one way or another. I'm smart enough to know what a jewel you are. In fact, I'd take you out to show my appreciation properly except that I'm tied up this weekend in a benefit golf tournament with some of the local sportscasters."

"Thanks for the thought, but I'm so tired I wouldn't be able to stay awake. I'm going home after work and crash."

"Go home right now. You've earned some rest." He took her hand in his and patted it, adding with a confident grin, "Take it easy this weekend and get some beauty sleep, because I have a hunch you're going to need it. Things could get pretty hectic after we get the Jason account."

Kate acted on Clint's suggestion gratefully, suddenly aware of how really tired she was from the pressure of the last busy weeks. At home, she sank down on the sofa, too weary even to change clothes. Surprisingly, she felt none of the exhilaration she should have felt upon hearing Clint's praise. Even his mention of her possible promotion hadn't particularly excited her. Maybe she was just tired, or maybe she was simply being cautious. After all, talking about a promotion was no assurance that you'd actually get it—even if the agency should get the Jason account. It wasn't wise to count on anything until it actually came to pass.

But then, chiding herself for her lack of enthusiasm, she reminded herself that she ought to be pleased by Clint's expression of his appreciation, thrilled by even the prospect of getting the promotion for which she had worked so hard.

The trouble was, she finally admitted, that her success didn't seem complete. She wouldn't be able to fully enjoy it until she had shared it with Steve. The reward she really wanted was to hear him tell her she had done well.

She waited beside the telephone, eagerly waiting for it to ring, hoping Steve would call when he got home from his office. Time passed, however, and the telephone did not ring. Several times, she started to dial his number, but each time she checked her impulse. It wouldn't be the same if she had to telephone him. Perfunctory congratulations wouldn't do. He had to *want* to know the outcome of the meeting today; he had to be happy about her success.

It was nine o'clock before Kate realized that Steve was not going to call. Disappointed, she gave up her vigil and went to bed. As exhausted as she was, though, it was some time before she fell asleep. And her last waking thought was the forlorn wish that she had been able to share her news with Steve.

On Saturday Kate continued to wait impatiently, hoping Steve would call. When noon came, and she still had not heard from him, she made a determined decision. If he was not going to call her, then she would call him. This silence between them had gone on long enough.

It was some time before he answered the telephone. At the sound of his voice, Kate's courage faltered. Suddenly she could think of nothing to say. "It's Kate, Steve," she finally managed to blurt out. "I thought you might like to know that we gave our presentation for Jason Enterprises."

"I hope it came off well." His tone, though restrained, seemed to hold a sincere interest.

"Clint was pleased with it. He feels we have a good chance of getting the account, and we're all pretty excited about it."

"I can imagine."

Kate paused, hoping that Steve would suggest seeing her that evening. When he said nothing more, she ventured timidly, "I wondered if you were planning to go to church in the morning."

"I always do." He hesitated and then asked tentatively, "Would you like to go, too?"

"Very much." Kate was too proud to add that she would also like very much to see him.

"Then why don't we go to the late service? We could have lunch after church if you'd like."

There was a studied courtesy in his voice that Kate did not know how to cope with. "That would be very nice," she said and then added a bit awkwardly, "I've a lot to tell you—about the project and all."

"I'll be interested in hearing about it."

He seemed distant, detached, and Kate could not

help but feel rejected. "Well, I guess I'll see you in the morning," she said, unable to find anything more to say.

She turned away from the phone, disappointed in the stilted conversation. Steve hadn't sounded like himself at all. There was a reserve in his tone that made him seem almost like a stranger. She decided unhappily that there could be only one explanation for his coolness toward her. He was still put out about her trip to Houston.

Well, tomorrow things were going to be different. Tomorrow she would make him understand. They would have the whole day to be together, and there would be plenty of time to straighten things out between them.

On Sunday morning, Kate was ready for church long before it was time for Steve to arrive. In her eagerness to see him, she was impatient for their day together to begin.

She dressed with special care, choosing a lightweight wool suit in a becoming shade of blue. A brightly patterned sweater accented it nicely. The jacket would be warm enough for the chill of the October morning, and the sweater and skirt would make a comfortable costume for anything Steve might suggest doing after lunch.

Assuming that he suggested spending the afternoon with her, Kate reminded herself. Considering his puzzling behavior recently, who could say what course the day would take? She hoped she would be able to restore at least some of the harmony which had once existed between them. But whatever happened, she intended to find out what had prompted his sudden disinterest in her, however painful the knowledge might be.

When he arrived, looking astonishingly handsome in a Harris tweed blazer and flannel slacks, Kate greeted him nervously, and there was a moment of strain between them as they set out for church. She was reluctant to ask him about the events of the past week, not wanting to seem to be prying. He, in turn, asked nothing about her week, and she was hesitant to introduce the subject of her job.

When they were seated in the church sanctuary, however, the tension between them relaxed. Entering the church, Kate experienced a feeling of coming home. In the now familiar surroundings, a feeling of well-being came over her. It was good to be here with Steve, sharing these special moments with him and with these others who had come to worship.

After the service, they lingered to visit with some of the churchgoers with whom they had by now become acquainted. Their drive to lunch was occupied by an animated discussion of the sermon and the news of various church activities. By the time they reached the restaurant Steve had chosen, they had reestablished the congeniality that usually existed between them.

They spent a pleasant hour over lunch. Kate waited until they had finished their dessert to tell Steve about the changes in her job.

"I thought you might be interested to know that there are going to be some changes at the office if we get the Jason account," she said, feeling a bit self-conscious to be bringing up the subject. "I don't know yet exactly what Clint has in mind, but I think he plans to take on some new people. So I expect he'll also make some changes in our assignments."

He smiled. "Is that a modest way of telling me that you're getting a promotion?"

"Clint mentioned the possibility. He didn't go into detail, of course, so I don't really know anything about it yet. But I feel sure there will be a change in my duties if we get the account."

"For the better, I trust."

"I should think so. With a larger staff, the pace ought to be more relaxed."

"Which means you'll limit yourself to working nights and rushing through supermarkets and eating peanut butter sandwiches," he said, laughing. "I'm afraid that, for you, work is like mowing a lawn in summertime. The grass keeps growing no matter how often you cut it."

"I'm not a make-work person," Kate protested, stung by his comment.

"I didn't say you were. I'm only saying that there will always be work to be done, and you'll always want to be the one to do it. You work because it's what you enjoy doing."

"It's not quite that simple, Steve," Kate said, earnestly seeking to make him understand. "At the present, my job demands a good deal from me, but I get to do a level of work with this agency that I would be very unlikely to have the chance to do anywhere else. In time, I expect to have more control over my schedule, but for the time being I have to work at the agency's pace."

"And you have every right to make that decision. You don't owe anybody an explanation for the choice you've made."

"But that doesn't mean I've chosen not to do anything but work. There are other—" Kate hesitated, not knowing exactly how to phrase her thoughts. "I intend to make time in my life for other things, too," she finished.

"Except that when it comes down to a choice, your work will always come first with you."

Kate looked at him with troubled eyes, wanting to make him understand the conflict she struggled with but unable to completely understand it herself.

As she groped for a way to express her feelings, he covered her hand with his and said kindly, "It's all right, Kate. I understand. You have to do what you think is right for you." He pushed his chair back from the table then, putting an end to the conversation. "And having a free afternoon, I think we need to be making the most of it. Why don't we drive out to the lake and enjoy the outdoors. Both of us could use some relaxation."

Kate had no choice but to drop the subject. During their drive to the lake, he resisted her efforts to reopen their discussion. But he was as amiable as always. By the time they returned to Kate's apartment late in the afternoon, their relationship seemed to be back on a relaxed, companionable basis.

To Kate's disappointment, though, Steve refused her invitation to supper, explaining that he had to make rounds at the hospital. But he paused at the door to ask, as an afterthought, "Shall we try to make it to church again next Sunday?"

"I'd love to. You know I enjoy being with you," Kate said quickly, trying to make her meaning as clear as she dared.

"I enjoy being with you, Kate. Very much," he said softly. He lifted a hand as if to touch her cheek, but then dropped it to his side and said jokingly, "Try to resist building too many empires this week."

Not knowing how to answer, Kate could only let him walk away. But as he passed beneath her window on the way to his car, she watched him pensively. She knew that some deeper emotion lay behind his light manner, but she didn't know how to get through to it. While he still seemed willing to offer her his friendship, he had thrown up a wall between them. He was withholding the warm affection they had previously shared.

Wistfully, she thought back to those tender moments, wondering if she would ever find the way to recall them.

The next week was a time of uncertainty for Kate. Routine at the office was unsettled while the staff waited for the decision on the Jason account. Her personal life was equally unsettled, her relationship with Steve remaining a puzzle. When Tuesday, his day off, passed without a call from him, her spirits drooped. There could be no doubt now that his feelings for her had changed. And when Friday came and there still had been no word from him, she decided forlornly that there wasn't going to be any.

She was getting ready to leave the office that afternoon when Clint called a meeting in his office. Sally Hines caught up with Kate just as she reached Clint's office door. Doug Siegel and Seth Barrow had already arrived. Clint was seated at his desk, his expression grave.

He waited until they were seated. Then solemnly he began. "I've had a call from Jason Enterprises, and they've made their decision. I'm going to meet with their representatives next week and work out the details of the contract." He waited a moment for his words to take effect, and then broke into a broad grin. "We've done it! We've got the account! They loved our presentation!"

There was a moment of pandemonium as the members of the team congratulated one another excitedly. Clint jumped to his feet and came around his desk to shake hands with Doug and Seth. He gave Sally a hug and, taking Kate in his arms, spun her around. "We did it, Kate, just as I said we would."

After a few more minutes of excited chatter, the group broke up to carry the good news to the rest of the staff. But as Kate started to leave, Clint detained her. "You know what this means, Kate. I meant what I said the other day. I intend to reorganize the executive structure of the agency, and there's going to be a real promotion in this for you. Of course, it will mean harder work and more responsibility, but you never let that stop you." He put his arm around her waist and pulled her close to him. "You're quite a woman, Kate. You've got what it takes to make it in this business. And we are going to succeed, Kate; we're going to do it together." He looked down at her in admiration, his eyes bright with determination. "You and I, little darlin', have only begun. We're going to the very top rung of the ladder."

There was a glitter of excitement in his eyes, and Kate sensed that he was letting her see a part of himself that he guarded closely. The intensity in his expression relaxed then, and his customary poise returned. "I'm not sure how long it will be before the contract is finalized. But as soon as it's signed, we'll talk about that promotion of yours. So get all your accounts in the best order you can, and be thinking about the kind of help you'll need when we increase your duties." He regarded her indulgently. "It's a big step you're taking, Kate. But you've got what it takes to succeed. You've got the drive and the commitment. And you're willing to make the sacrifices it takes to be a success."

Kate left the office in a daze, overwhelmed by Clint's announcement, not quite able to grasp the significance. But that night, as she thought back over their conversation and the reality of it became clear to her, she pondered it with some apprehension. Did she have the commitment Clint talked about? Was she, indeed, ready to give up everything in her life to her job? Now that the choice confronted her, how much was she willing to sacrifice for success?

On Saturday night, Clint held a party for the staff members assigned to the Jason account. Held at a private club he belonged to, it was a lavish affair. He had spared no expense and overlooked no detail in making the evening a memorable one. It was a fitting tribute to a successful effort, but it also ushered in a new era for the Hansen Agency. Late in the evening, Kate was given her first inkling of what the future might hold for her.

She and Clint were sitting at the end of the table, apart from the other guests. He leaned close to her and said in a confidential tone, "Aren't you the least bit curious about your new assignment, Kate?"

"Of course I'm curious. But I've learned to be patient where your plans are concerned. I know I won't find out anything until you're ready to tell me."

He laughed, seeming pleased. "You read me very well." He studied her in appraisal. "That's one of your strongest points, as a matter of fact. You read people very well."

Kate could think of a certain doctor she couldn't read at all. How right Clint was about her insight into their clients, she couldn't say.

"That's why," Clint continued, pausing for emphasis, "I've decided to make you an Account Executive."

Kate's eyes widened. Such a title would put her in a senior position with the agency, just below Clint in the organization, a position he had up to now refused to bestow on anyone.

His smile broadened as he watched her reaction. "I rather thought that might jolt you a bit."

"I don't know what to think about it," Kate exclaimed.

"That it's a fantastic opportunity and you're straining the leash to get at it, of course." Clint's expression intensified. "I see it this way, Kate. You and I make a fantastic team. I can turn up potential clients as well as anyone in the business, and you've got a sixth sense about what it takes to bring in an account. If I can give you the people you need to do the work, I know we can double the size of this agency within a few years."

"What about the art work, the copy, all the rest of

the work that goes into developing an idea? How could I possibly get it all done?"

"You couldn't. You'd assign all the basic work to someone else. You'd be an executive, love, and executives delegate. They learn to use other people's brain power." A calculating look came into his eyes. "You know, of course, that I can't make you the lone Account Executive. Even if you could handle all the accounts, it would be too obvious if I singled you out for such a promotion. I plan to make Doug Siegel Account Executive, too. With the two of you to supervise the work, we can increase our workload tremendously."

"But I like doing the detailed work of developing an idea," Kate said, a bit dubious as she began to perceive his intent.

"You have to grow, Kate," he said impatiently. "You can't hang onto every little detail of the work. You learn to delegate as you move up."

"Project development is what I do best, though."

Clint shook his head. "What you do best, love, is client contact. You know instinctively what clients want and how to give it to them. And I want to make use of that ability. It's a waste to have you spending your time dawdling over drawings and copy. I want you working with me. Together, there's no limit to what we can do."

Kate's doubts began to surface. If Clint was thinking of more time spent entertaining people, she could find little enthusiasm for the prospect. She was already burdened with that sort of the thing to the limit of her endurance.

"To be honest, Clint," she began uncertainly, "I was hoping to have a bit more free time. I've been working pretty close to the wire for some time now."

His eyes narrowed. "I don't know exactly what you mean by 'free time,' Kate. What is it exactly that you're trying to say?"

"It's this matter of business entertaining, Clint," Kate said, gathering her courage. "It's very nice and all, but a person has to have some time for personal things."

"Things or someone?" He leveled a penetrating glance at her. "I've been aware that you're seeing someone, Kate. Your unexplained absences haven't deceived me in the least. And, whoever the man is, I don't blame him for wanting to have you to himself. You're a beautiful woman and an intriguing person. It's to be expected that men are going to be attracted to you."

"Then you do understand?" Kate's hope soared.

"I understand perfectly and, frankly, as a result am hurrying developments along a little bit." He picked up her hand and cradled it in his. "I think you know there isn't a place for another man in your life. I think you know by now that my interest in you isn't entirely platonic, even though I've never expressed my feelings. I've been waiting until the right time because I knew you weren't ready to handle an emotional involvement. I've watched you develop from an eager, talented girl into an assured, capable woman—the woman I've looked for and waited for." His voice softened, his tone taking on an intimacy. A possessiveness came into his eyes.

"We're right for each other, Kate. You've got everything I want in a woman. Beauty, intelligence, poise—and most of all, ambition. You're smart enough to want the excitement, the prestige, the pressure of standing off the competition, and you're woman enough to know how to savor the rewards of success. We're good together, Kate, and not just in business. We can go to the top together. We can have it all. What I'm saying," he finished, squeezing her hand tightly, "is that I want us to be a team in every way. How does Clint & Kate Hansen, Associates, sound to you?"

As he gazed at her expectantly, Kate was too startled to react.

Her thoughts in a whirl, she was struck dumb by this sudden expression of his feelings. Such a possibility had never occurred to her.

The last thing in the world she would have expected was that Clint Hansen would want to marry her.

CHAPTER 11

FOR KATE, SUNDAY WAS a day of emotional turmoil. She could only view the proposed change in her job with confusion. As for Clint's proposal of marriage, she refused to even think about it. She couldn't believe he had been serious. He had simply been carried away in an expansive moment.

Nor did her day with Steve help her sort out her feelings. After church, Steve accepted an invitation to lunch with two of their fellow churchgoers, a friendly young married couple named Tim and Mary Carter. The Carters were engaging people, and under other circumstances Kate would have been pleased by their company. But today it meant she would have no chance to talk to Steve about personal matters.

As the day progressed, however, she decided it was probably just as well. Trying to talk to Steve would likely have only added to her problems. Her job was already a sore subject between them, and she could hardly tell him about Clint Hansen's proposal, particularly in view of the attitude Steve was displaying toward her. While he was considerate and congenial, he showed no trace of the romantic interest he had once expressed. Steve Turner, she finally decided, was more of an enigma to her than Clint. When he took her back to her apartment at midafternoon, she did not invite him in. Deeply hurt and disturbed, she was not up to any more emotional strain.

She spent the evening pondering her situation. How suddenly life could change! Only a few months ago she was secure in her work, certain of her plans for the future. Now she was totally confused. While it was flattering to be considered ready for the promotion to Account Executive, taking the job would mean giving up the part of her work she liked best, and she was not sure she was ready to do that.

Nor was she ready to deal with Clint's expression of personal interest in her. At one time, she might have felt complimented by a proposal of marriage from dynamic Clint Hansen. Now she had to wonder how much she and Clint actually had in common. Although she admired his compelling personality and his shrewdness in business, she had come to seriously question his methods. While Clint could never be labeled unethical, she had to wonder at his values. She couldn't believe that parties and social contacts were as important as he insisted. Ultimately, success in business came down to your performance in your job. Flattery could never take the place of honesty in business dealings, nor could extravagant entertaining substitute for quality work.

These convictions made her all the more troubled about the promotion Clint had talked about, more uncertain as to whether she wanted it. Certainly she didn't want all the socializing that went with it. Maybe that was the real problem, she thought, troubled. Maybe she didn't want the sophisticated lifestyle that was so important to Clint.

At the same time, the mystifying status of her relationship with Steve did nothing to simplify her decision. She was at a loss to explain his puzzling behavior. He seemed to have changed completely in his feelings for her. While he acted as though he wanted to continue their friendship, at the same time he was drawing away from her. Only a fool, she told herself bitterly, would let herself fall more deeply in love with a man who cared for her only as a friend.

Her concerns still weighed heavily upon her the following morning. With considerable nervousness, she answered Clint's summons to his office, wondering what to expect and how she was to respond to him.

He greeted her warmly with no trace of discomposure. Taking her hands in his, he smiled down at her, and she noticed a provocative twinkle in his eyes. "I hope you noticed that I left you completely to yourself yesterday. I thought you might need some time to think. I realize that I gave you a lot to think about Saturday night."

Kate managed a wan smile. "You never do things halfway."

Her answer seemed to please him. "It's not my style. I believe in going for the brass ring—or, more precisely, the pot of gold. Why settle for half when you can have it all?" His expression became guarded then, and he regarded her solemnly.

"Of course, it will be awhile before the things we talked about can take place. Everything I said to you has got to be kept in confidence until the time is right. If my plans leaked out, it would cause a considerable stir here at the office, and I think you'll agree that we don't want to rock the boat right now."

"Definitely not," Kate said, relieved to have been given a reprieve.

"I knew I could count on your understanding," he said with satisfaction. "That's what I like best about you, Kate. You've got a sensible head on your shoulders. You think like a man."

"Do I?" Kate wasn't sure she ought to feel complimented.

"We'll have to keep your promotion confidential until I'm ready to announce all the organizational changes," he warned. "We don't want Doug Siegel to start off feeling that you've got the inside track."

"As a matter of fact, I'm quite concerned about the reaction of all the other people in the office," Kate said, feeling pushed to a conclusion she wasn't ready to make. "I haven't been with the firm nearly as long as many of them. They might resent my being given such a promotion."

His expression sharpened. "I don't *give* promotions, Kate. People earn them. Everybody in this office knows that. As for our personal relationship, I think you'll agree that we should keep it just that way. Very personal and very private. Just between the two of us for the present. We've got a lot to accomplish in the next few months, and we don't want a lot of office gossip getting in our way."

"I quite agree," Kate said quickly, wanting to put the brakes on this situation that was developing far too fast to suit her liking. "In fact . . ."

"You don't have to say it, Kate," he said with a perceptive smile. "I realize that you're a bit overwhelmed by all this. After all, I am a bit ahead of you. And I don't want to do anything precipitously. We've got to move slowly and carefully in going public with our relationship, let people gradually get used to us as a team. Otherwise, it would be very disruptive to us, both personally and professionally."

"I definitely need to think about this," Kate said, sparring for time.

"Time to get used to it," he corrected her. Then, slipping an arm around her shoulders, he gave her an affectionate hug. "And while you're about it, both of us have a lot of work to do. Important work that won't keep. So we'll just keep the lid on our news for awhile. Agreed?"

Kate barely nodded and retreated hastily, relieved that she was to have time to sort things out. She still could not believe Clint was thinking seriously of marriage. And she certainly wasn't ready to consider such a commitment. She wasn't even sure yet what she thought about being Account Executive. There were simply too many decisions for her to cope with at once.

After work that evening, however, when she had time to think over her conversation with Clint, Kate realized she had to take hold of her own affairs. She couldn't afford to drift, leaving it to Clint to act however he might choose. She had to know what she wanted and what she was willing to do. Otherwise, she risked being swept along by the strength of Clint's wishes, regardless of what her own desires might be.

Unhappily, Steve Turner still figured heavily in those desires, however pointlessly. Although he showed every sign of a man who had lost interest in her, Kate wasn't ready to put him out of her life. She had found a relationship with him unlike any she had ever experienced; he held an attraction for her she couldn't deny. She had fallen in love with him, and her feelings weren't like water flowing through a faucet to be turned on and off at will.

Steve had said he cared for her and had asked her to make a place in her life for him. If his feelings for her had changed, she had to know why. She couldn't get on with her life as long as she was clinging to the hope that he still cared for her.

Gathering her courage, she called Steve. Tomorrow night was his evening off, and she intended to invite him to dinner. He could consider her forward if he liked, but she was determined to take matters in hand. She was going to put an end to this uncertainty.

Luckily, she found him at home. He seemed pleased by her invitation and accepted it readily. *Exasperating man,* she thought as she looked accusingly at the telephone. Why did he have to be so contradictory?

She managed to get home from work promptly the next day, thanks to Clint's preoccupation with his own pressing business. With a little thought, she was able to put together a simple meal. Steve could make all the jokes he wanted to about prepared foods, but they were the answer to a working girl's prayers. Small strips of beef sirloin browned with a package of stir-fry vegetables made a nice dish served over quick-cooked rice. She added a fresh fruit salad and packaged rolls, topping off the meal with caramel sundaes. No feast but certainly an adequate offering, she assured herself as she hurriedly freshened her appearance.

Steve seemed to approve of her efforts. He ate hungrily, complimenting her afterward on the meal. "A person would never guess that you had done a hard day's work before putting together a spread like this," he told her.

"I know a few shortcuts," Kate confessed.

"Then I wish you'd tell me about them. I've spent my day off doing laundry and cleaning the apartment. I'm afraid I'm not very handy at that sort of thing," he confessed.

"I thought the efficient Dr. Turner was an expert at just about everything," Kate teased.

"Hardly," he said ruefully. "I can bumble my way through the cleaning, but somehow I can't get the hang of folding clothes. I'm developing a deep respect for the vanishing profession of housewife. I don't seem to be able to develop the knack for it."

Kate laughed. "Somehow you do seem more suited to a white coat than an apron."

"And here I was thinking how well that apron suited you," he replied, looking across the table at the cobbler's smock she had slipped on to protect her white silk blouse.

Kate removed the apron hastily. "I forgot to take it off after I served dinner," she exclaimed.

"I thought it was very becoming," he said, a bit wistfully. An oddly vulnerable expression crossed his face fleetingly, disappearing as he rose purposefully from the table. "And to prove that I can show off an apron as well as the next man, I insist on doing the dishes."

"Absolutely not," Kate said, blowing out the candles determinedly. "We're not going to spend your evening off in the kitchen."

She led him to the living room sofa and sat down beside him, adjusting the cushions so that she sat facing him. "Now, tell me what you've been doing with yourself. We don't seem to see all that much of each other these days."

"I'm well aware of that, Kate," he said.

His candor was disconcerting. Kate was not sure she had the courage to question his meaning. If he was saying that he had deliberately avoided seeing her, she wasn't sure she was ready to hear it. With forced cheerfulness, she said, "Then let's catch up on the news."

"There isn't much. I've been working some pretty long hours since Dr. Wallace's illness."

"I didn't know he was ill," Kate said, concerned. "I hope it isn't serious."

"He has a mild heart condition that flared up recently. A warning to him to slow down. He's feeling fine now and fortunately can be treated with medication—along with a more sensible schedule. He can't keep on working the long, tiring hours he has put in for so many years."

"Unfortunately, a doctor's life is a demanding one," Kate said sympathetically. She cast a reflective glance at Steve. "You know, you really haven't the right to scold me about my workload. You put in some very long hours yourself."

"I realize that, Kate," he said, suddenly solemn. "I mean, I've had a chance to think about it, and I admit that I had no right to take it upon myself to tell you how to live."

"I never took it that way," Kate said quickly.

"Still, I can see that I intruded upon your life—however well-meaning I might have been—and you have every right to resent it."

"I didn't resent it. I was grateful for your—" Kate hesitated, suddenly shy, and then finished awkwardly, "for your friendship."

His expression was unreadable as he said softly, "My friendship, Kate?"

Not able to guess his meaning, she rushed ahead. "It has meant a great deal to me, Steve. That's why I invited you over tonight. A lot is going on in my life right now, and I need to talk to you."

She waited for a response from him, some sign of encouragement. But he said nothing, and his expression gave her no clue as to his thoughts. The silence between them deepened as she searched for a tactful way to pursue the subject she was determined to discuss. It was a relief when the doorbell sounded, interrupting the awkward moment.

Expecting to see the boy who delivered the newspaper or some other casual caller who could be dispatched promptly, she hurried to the door. Instead, to her dismay, she found that she had a visitor. Standing at the door, smiling at her expectantly, was Clint Hansen.

Not waiting for an invitation, he strode into the room. "I came by to continue the conversation we had this morning. We've still a good many things to talk about, but the office was hardly the place for such personal matters," he said, dropping a possessive arm around Kate's shoulders.

Then, catching sight of Steve, he stopped abruptly. His glance swept around the apartment, taking in the dining nook where the table still bore the traces of dinner, and finally settling accusingly upon Kate. "I seem to be interrupting something. Perhaps you should introduce me to your guest. I don't believe we've had the occasion to meet."

Kate was struck dumb. Clint never dropped in without calling first. Why, of all nights, had he chosen to break his pattern on this one? Clumsily, she managed to make the introductions. "Clint, this is my—my friend, Dr. Steve Turner. Steve, this is Clint Hansen, my boss."

Steve stood and acknowledged the introduction with studied courtesy, his face expressionless. Clint's arm finally fell from Kate's shoulders, and he leveled an icy glance at her. "Don't you think that designation is a bit heavy, love? I'd say that I was a bit more to you than your boss."

"Steve has heard me talk about you—about my job," Kate said with a sinking heart. This encounter was not going well at all.

"I don't believe I've heard you mention Dr. Turner, though," Clint commented in clipped tones, confirming her fears.

"Actually, we met in a rather amusing way," Kate said, laughing nervously. "Steve is my doctor—or at least he is now. I met him when I went to see my regular doctor and Steve was taking his place."

Clint seemed to find no amusement in Kate's explanation. "I wasn't aware that you had been ill."

"Just some headaches."

"Then you should have told me. I certainly don't want you trying to work when you're not feeling well." Clint smiled frostily at Steve. "Kate goes a bit out of her way not to take advantage of her situation at the agency—which is, as she may have told you, somewhat privileged."

"Aside from the fact that she works long hours, Kate has told me very little about her situation at work," Steve said tersely.

"I wasn't referring to her job but to our relationship." Clint shot a piercing glance at Kate. "I hope Dr. Turner's visit tonight doesn't mean you have medical problems you haven't told me about."

"Of course not," Kate said impatiently. How dare Clint imply a relationship between them that until a few days ago hadn't even been mentioned, much less agreed to—at least, on her part. And until she committed herself to him—which at this moment there was little chance of her doing—he had no claim on her at all. It was unforgivable of him to suggest that he did. Casting a reproving glance at him, she said, "Steve's visit tonight is entirely a social one, Clint."

Clint glared at her with stony disapproval, his anger barely concealed. "In that case, I'll leave you to it. You and I will see each other tomorrow. But we do have things to talk about." With a few barely polite words to Steve and another reproachful glance at Kate, he left abruptly, slamming the door behind him.

Kate stood for a moment, looking helplessly at Steve. How could she explain the truth about Clint's insinuations? "Things aren't quite as they seem, Steve," she began unhappily as they resumed their seats on the sofa. "As a matter of fact, Clint was part of what I wanted to talk to you about. I'm having some problems that I don't know exactly how to deal with."

His lips twisted into a wry smile, but his bleak and accusing eyes held no humor. "It seems to me that you have matters under control."

"Things are completely *out* of control. Everything is happening so fast I don't know what to do about it," Kate burst out. "Clint has offered me a promotion to Account Executive, and I'm not even sure I want the job. And on top of it he takes it for granted that we—that he and I—" Her voice faltered as she found it difficult to say the words.

"I think you had better finish," Steve said soberly.

"He's talking as though we were getting married. And there has never been anything like that between Clint and me. I admire him professionally, and we work well together. But I've never thought of him in a—a romantic way before."

"But how do you feel about him now, Kate?"

She looked at him bleakly. "I don't want to think about him. What about us, Steve? What about you and me? I have to know what has happened to change things between us."

"Nothing has changed, at least as far as I'm concerned."

"Except that you never call me anymore or seem to want to see me," Kate said.

He stared down at the floor, seeming to weigh a decision. Finally, with difficulty, he said, "I thought about where we were heading, Kate, and I realized I was being very selfish. I've been asking you to change your life to accommodate mine, and I see that I haven't the right to ask that of you."

"Of course you do. If two people want to be together, they have to make changes to accommodate each other," Kate protested.

"That's just the point. I'm a doctor with a first commitment to my patients. There's very little accommodating that I can do. Yet I'm asking you to accept my schedule at the expense of a job that means as much to you as mine does to me."

"I understand that your responsibilities come first, Steve, and it really isn't all that difficult to adjust to them. I got very busy for awhile, but I told you things would be different as soon as we settled the Jason account."

He shook his head. "It appears to me that there's a lot more involved than an agency account—or even your job. It comes down to what we want out of life. The way you seem to want to live your life is very different from the way I want to live mine."

"I don't see that there's anything so terribly wrong about the way I live," Kate replied, taken aback.

"I didn't say there was." He ran a hand through his hair unhappily. "I'm basically a slow-track guy, Kate. I'm not a sophisticated man like Clint. I can't offer you excitement or status or an extravagant lifestyle. I don't want to build the biggest and most lucrative practice in town. I just want to be the best doctor I can and lead a simple Christian life."

"But I want to live a Christian life, too. You know I don't care anything about social status or money. I'll admit I spend more time at social events than I care to, and some of the people I associate with have far different standards than mine. But I don't let other people's standards affect mine. You might be surprised that I carry around a highball over the course of an evening without so much as taking a sip," Kate defended herself.

"That's equivocating, Kate," he said impatiently. "If you don't want the highball, why do you feel obliged to carry it around?"

His question took Kate by surprise. She had no ready answer.

He sighed unhappily. "I don't mean to judge you, Kate. It's up to you to decide what you do. But I do believe a person has to live up to his own values."

"I do live up to my values," Kate cried out, rankled by his implied criticism.

"I'm not suggesting that you don't," he said wearily. "But I have to admit that I have trouble coping with your seemingly boundless ambition."

Kate was mystified by his comment. "There's nothing wrong with wanting to succeed at your work."

"I guess that depends on what you're willing to do to succeed and what you consider to be success. And I have to wonder if there isn't a great deal of difference between your idea of success and mine."

His eyes were filled with unhappiness, but his expression was unyielding. "You told me you had to get your priorities straightened out, and I have to agree with you. Under the circumstances, I thought it was best to give you some space."

"But how can I do anything about priorities when I don't know how I stand with you?" Kate demanded in frustration.

He gazed at her steadily. "I won't be an alternative to Clint," he said at last. "You're going to have to make up your mind whether you want what he has to offer you. Until you know what you want and how you plan to go about getting it, you and I don't have much to talk about."

"I can't very well plan my life if I don't even know who is going to be part of it," Kate protested angrily.

"I think that depends on you, Kate."

"Not entirely." Kate's eyes beseeched him. "I could use a little input from you."

A mask dropped over his face in resistance to her plea. "I can't help you make this decision, Kate. You have to decide for yourself what you want out of life." He gazed at her sadly for a moment and then, pressing a gentle kiss to her forehead, rose to go.

Desolately, Kate listened to the door close behind him, to the sound of his footsteps fading away. As the heavy silence of the apartment closed in around her, she asked herself helplessly what decision there was for her to make. What difference did it make what she wanted her life to be when it seemed that Steve didn't want to be part of it?

CHAPTER 12

KATE ARRIVED AT HER OFFICE the following morning in dismal spirits. It was a gray, rainy day as dreary as her state of mind. During the long night, she had come to a kind of acceptance of Steve's seeming rejection of her. For it was a rejection, however kindly put—a rejection of her values and a condemnation of her goals.

The difficult evening hadn't been helped any by Clint's untimely arrival. Or by his intimation that there was a personal relationship between them. Kate had given him no indication to suggest such a thing; in fact, thinking of him romantically was such a completely new idea to her that she had hardly had time to think about it at all. Events were moving far too fast. Clint was simply taking over her life without any consideration of her own wishes.

Still angry, Kate avoided seeing Clint for most of the morning. When, just before lunch, he requested that she come to his office, she did so reluctantly. Considering last night's incident, Clint could hardly be expected to be in the best of moods, and she was still too resentful to cope with any more of his overbearing, dictatorial ways.

To her surprise, Clint was in the most conciliatory frame of mind. He was even a bit contrite. "I suppose I owe you an explanation for bursting in on you as I did last night," he said. "I didn't stop to think that you might have a visitor."

"You could have telephoned first," she suggested icily.

He shrugged apologetically. "I know. I realized after I left that I haven't given you time to adjust to our new relationship. I was aware that you were seeing someone, and it's unreasonable to think there won't be some loose ends for you to take care of."

"It isn't a question of loose ends, Clint," Kate objected. "We haven't even had a chance to discuss any of this."

"And we did agree to put things on hold for awhile. It's obviously going to take a little time to work things out." He offered her a placating smile. "I won't rush you, Kate. Take time to get used to the idea."

"It's going to take some time—and some thought, Clint. This is all very new to me."

"I know. It goes against all my convictions. I've always believed that my business and personal life should be kept completely separate. But working with you has changed my mind, Kate." His voice was low and persuasive. "You know, we really do make a great team."

Looking at Clint, Kate had to admit that most women would find him appealing. He was handsome, intelligent, exciting. His enthusiasm and self-confidence seemed contagious. When she was with Clint, she felt she could accomplish anything. And, regardless of their differences in viewpoint, Clint wasn't an immoral man. He was simply overzealous in his ambitions. Thinking rebelliously of Steve's condemnation of her own ambitions, she smiled at Clint. "I guess we do make a good team, don't we?"

"The best." His eyes glowed with a sudden intensity as he reached for her hands and clasped them tightly. "We can have it all, you and I—the challenge, the excitement, all the rewards of success. We can do it, Kate. We can go to the top together."

A wave of excitement swept over Kate as she listened to him. There was a heady exhilaration in the drive and ambition this man possessed. "You make it sound so easy, Clint," she murmured.

"You just have to want it enough to go after it, Kate. Think about it." He released her hands then and assumed his usual suave manner. "In the meantime, there are other things to occupy us. I've got some rather exciting news. What would you say if I told you we'd had a nibble from a major product distributor?" he asked, watching her expectantly.

"I'd wonder what we could possibly do about it, considering the workload at the agency right now."

He waggled a finger at her. "Think positively, Kate. You don't turn down a chance like this. You go after it."

"But we aren't even geared up to handle the Jason account yet. How could we possibly take on anything more?"

"By the time we could generate the kind of interest we need to make a real try, we'll have the Jason account well under way and however large a staff we need to move on." His eyes glittered with excitement. "Don't you understand, Kate? We're in the big time now. We'll be competing with the national firms on this one."

Kate could see that Clint's mind was already set on this new goal. The Jason account was behind him, and he was ready for another challenge. "I suppose the rest of us can manage to get the Jason account underway while you pursue this other one," she said, thinking aloud.

"Now you're using your head," he said approvingly. "I'm having lunch with one of their PR people today, and I'll try to set up dinner one night this week. Naturally, I'll want you along. I'll get back to you as soon as I know anything."

Kate left Clint's office, shaking her head in bemusement. He really was a most amazing man. Maybe she ought to consider his proposal. She could do far worse with her life. Indeed, most women would consider themselves lucky to be in her position. And if she and Clint differed in some of their ideas, she at least knew what to expect from him—which was more than she could say for Steve Turner. If she used her head instead of her heart, she would forget about Steve and his disapproval and think about making a life with Clint.

In the hectic days that followed, Kate had no time for thoughts of personal affairs. Her days began early and ended late. Her working hours were spent training the two assistants Clint had hired for her and reassigning to them the accounts she had previously worked on; the nights when she accompanied Clint on business engagements rarely ended before midnight. What few evenings she had free were spent developing her ideas for her part of the Jason account.

She refused to let herself think of Steve, whom she had not seen since the unhappy meeting between him and Clint. He had telephoned once, but their conversation was strained and unsatisfactory. He had not mentioned seeing her, even for church on Sunday, and she was too proud to suggest it. He had made it clear that he considered their lifestyles too different to be reconciled. Their relationship was over. She had to get on as best as she could with the life she knew.

Fortunately, she was not required to deal with her personal relationship with Clint. Their professional lives demanded all their time. Clint was busier than ever with his stepped-up plans for client acquisition, as he had labeled it. The rest of his time was spent reorganizing the agency and interviewing applicants for the new jobs he had created. Pressed to meet all her obligations, Kate put her personal life on hold.

She did take a few moments away from her responsibilities when Linda Grant telephoned unexpectedly one day. Pleased, Kate accepted her invitation to lunch at the Parkview Hotel where Linda worked.

The exclusive dining room at the Parkview was elegantly decorated. The soft music and attentive service was soothing and relaxing. "I'm glad you called. It has been too long since we've had a chance to talk," Kate said as she slipped into her chair across the table from Linda.

"Much too long," Linda agreed.

"Things have been moving so fast at the agency that I haven't had a free moment. There always seems to be one more thing that needs to be done. But then I suppose that's part of the business. I expect you're as busy as I am."

Linda grinned. "I've found the job grows to take up about as much time as you'll let it. For myself, I'm slacking off a bit. I'm making some time for little old Linda."

"Do I take it that there is a special reason behind that decision?" Observing Linda's reaction, Kate added, "Or perhaps a special person?"

"Most definitely. He's an absolute dream. His name is Mike Donley, and he's a veterinarian. I met him when I took my cat in for her shots. I bought the cat for company. Little did I guess that the company would end up being Mike."

Linda's glowing expression left no doubt that someone very special had come into her life. "I'm really happy for you," Kate told her. "I hope things work out well for the two of you."

"Oh, they will. I'm going to see that they do. I've waited a long time for Mike to come along."

"Now I know why I haven't seen anything of you lately," Kate teased. "You've practically vanished from the social scene. How have you been able to avoid the openings and press parties and all?"

"I only go to the ones that my job absolutely requires."

"Does Mike understand about your job?"

"Completely. I take him along with me to the press parties I have to attend, and he manages to enjoy them. He says it's good to be around creatures that talk instead of bark."

"You're a lucky girl, then," Kate commented with a twinge of envy. "Lots of men can't—or won't—cope with the demands of a woman's job."

"Mike is very understanding about my work, thank goodness. But I'll have to say, I've cut down on its demands. I earn my paycheck and then some, but I don't let my job take up all my time." Linda paused, and her cheery expression faded. "Actually, though, it's your job I wanted to talk about, Kate."

"Mine?" Kate was taken by surprise.

Linda hesitated and then plunged in determinedly. "I hope you won't be offended or think I'm meddling. And I want to make it clear that I'm doing this on my own. Nobody at Jason Enterprises has asked me to talk to you. In fact, I would probably be in trouble if anybody found out about it. But I like you a lot, Kate, and I think we're good enough friends that you'll understand my concern."

"Concern about what?" Kate asked, bewildered.

"The word is out in our PR department that Clint has taken you off the Jason account. Is it true?"

"Of course he hasn't. I'm working on it very hard, as a matter of fact."

Linda gave a sigh of relief. "I'm glad to hear it because, frankly, there has been quite a bit of concern. Maybe I'm talking out of turn, but I know you'll respect my confidence. And I think you ought to know that your ideas were the reason Clint's agency got the account. There have been rumors about all the changes Clint's making at the agency, and our people have gotten a little antsy. They wouldn't take it very well if you were taken off the account."

"Clint's making some organizational changes and taking on some new people, but I'm doing the development on your account—my part of it, at least."

"Then I'll quit worrying," Linda said with an apologetic smile. "It's just that I felt I would be less than a friend if I didn't warn you. Clint's got to deliver what he promised, or he'll be in trouble."

"Oh, he will. Clint knows the success of the agency depends on the quality of the work we do."

"Still, you'll admit he moves pretty fast. And trying to do too much too soon can be a mistake."

"Clint looks ahead, of course. All successful people do," Kate said, defending him. "But he won't stint on the quality of the work he does."

"Then if anybody brings it up, I'll pass the word that the changes at the Hansen Agency don't mean anything as far as you're concerned."

It was Kate's turn to hesitate. "Clint hasn't announced exactly what he plans to do, but there may be some changes in titles—that kind of thing. But nothing that should affect the Jason account."

"Does that mean you're in for one of those changes in title?" Linda observed Kate curiously.

"As I said, things are still pretty much up in the air." Kate felt obligated to evade Linda's question. And her answer was true. No definite decisions had been made as far as she was concerned, although she felt sure Linda would be surprised at the changes that were being considered. She felt a sudden, urgent need to talk to someone about it all—her job, her relationship with Clint, her feelings for him.

"Then something is in the wind," Linda said, observing her speculatively. "I take it from your heavy silence that it isn't anything you can discuss."

"I only wish I could, because I could use a sympathetic ear. Things are moving awfully fast for me these days," Kate said with a sigh. "I can say, though, that whatever happens won't affect the Jason account."

"Then I'll drop the subject. But before we leave it, I'd like to say one thing—in case it should ever make a difference. Not that it's likely to happen, but just in case you should ever think about leaving the Hansen Agency, you could write your own ticket at Jason Enterprises. They love your work, Kate." Linda's expression brightened. "And that's enough of that kind of talk. Wouldn't you like to hear some more about Mike?"

The rest of their time together passed pleasantly. Linda's conversation, dotted with references to Mike, was filled with good humor. Kate returned to the office, her spirits lightened by the enjoyable lunch hour. Linda Grant was fun to be with. More important, she was a good friend.

Linda's warning about the Jason account was troubling to Kate, though. She couldn't help feeling a bit uneasy about the reassurances she had given Linda. While Clint's plans would in no way interfere with the agency's handling of the account, an outsider might get a false picture. Some of the changes he had in mind might arouse questions about the workings of the agency.

Kate wavered, trying to decide on the right course to follow. Although she would never betray Linda's confidence, if there was any problem concerning the Jason account, he ought to know it. He deserved some warning of any potential trouble he might be creating for himself with such an important client. The problem was how to tell him what she had learned without exposing Linda, how to bring up the subject in a diplomatic way.

Concerned though she was about her troublesome knowledge, Kate found no opportunity to talk about it to Clint. Both of them were totally occupied with their work. She saw little of him at the office. Almost every evening was devoted to business entertaining. She attended countless dinners, charitable events, receptions honoring company executives or prestigious visitors to the city, the opening of a chic new European-financed boutique, a showing of the newest collection of a famous designer's line of women's clothing. She decided wearily that if knowing people was the key to success, as Clint insisted it was, then the agency's future was secure. She felt as though she had surely by now met half the population of Dallas.

It was a fatiguing routine, one that Kate had no particular liking for. There was a facelessness about meeting people in such numbers. It was hard to remember which of them she had actually met and which she had only noticed somewhere in crowd. Clint was amazing in his ability to single out people and remember them in detail. It made it all the more difficult for him to understand the limitations of people like Kate.

It was also difficult to explain to him why she welcomed so gratefully the rare evenings she spent at home. "You work all day at the office; why would you want to work some more at night?" he reasoned. "I should think you would enjoy getting out and having some fun." He couldn't perceive that, to Kate, real pleasure came from the indulgence in quiet meditation, sketching out an idea, or maybe simply puttering about in her apartment.

Under the pressure of their busy schedules, Clint had said nothing more about any personal plans between them. The omission was brought home to her sharply late one Friday afternoon when Clint requested that she join him in his office.

Kate saw at once from his jaunty enthusiasm that something important was underway. He wasted no time getting to the source of his exultant mood. "Are you ready for some good news? I mean, big news—the kind that brings you out of your chair."

"It would depends on the news," Kate said warily.

"What if I told you we've got a very good chance at doing a presentation for that national food supply company I told you about?"

"I would wonder how we could possibly take on such a project with all the changes you're making at the agency right now," Kate replied.

"Kate, Kate, my overpractical little Kate. Where is your confidence?" he said with a despairing sigh. "What will it take for me to convince you that you have to be bold in this business? You can't rest on past accomplishments, waiting passively for something good to happen to you. You have to have vision, reach out for opportunities. You have to make things happen."

Kate leveled a mistrustful glance at him. "I just like to be sure I can handle what's already happening before I take on anything more."

"And we can. We have the staff now to handle the volume of work we've taken on, and I'm ready to move on. On Monday I intend to announce the promotions to Account Executive for you and Doug. At the same time, I want to announce the assignments you've made within your sections. With the organizational changes behind us, we'll be ready to tackle a new account."

"But we haven't even gotten the Jason account launched," Kate objected. "I still have a good deal of work to do on my end."

He shook his head. "Not you, Kate. I'm taking you off the Jason account and assigning it to Doug. You and I are going after the new one together."

Kate looked at him in dismay. "But I had counted on finishing my work on the Jason account. I have it all planned out."

"That's the point, Kate. Since you do have it all planned out, someone else can handle the details." He smiled at her persuasively. "Don't you understand? You're an executive now. You have to learn how to use other people's talents. Your job is going after new accounts."

"But the development part of the work is what I like best, Clint," Kate exclaimed.

"And development is what you'll be doing. Developing the ideas that will attract new accounts. You're my idea girl, Kate. You're too valuable to spend your time mulling over details. We've got other people who can do that very well—with your supervision, of course."

"But I won't even be supervising the work on the Jason account."

"It better fits my plans to have Doug supervise the development of the Jason account," Clint said, annoyed. "I had to draw lines somewhere in reorganizing. The realities of business are such that you can't be sentimental about assigning duties. You know that, Kate."

"But how will the Jason people feel about it?" Kate objected, recalling Linda Grant's warning.

"The internal structure of our agency isn't any of their business. They don't need to know who works on their account. We'll deliver the finished product they've been promised. That's all they're entitled to."

In her disappointment, Kate was at a loss for words. She had never guessed that Clint had planned such a drastic change in her duties. Nor could she help being disturbed about the Jason people's reaction. She had a terrible feeling that Clint was wrong in what he was doing.

"Don't look so downcast, Kate. You have to turn

loose of the past and look ahead to all the good things in the future," he consoled her, reaching out to take her by the arms and draw her close to him. "It's time for us to move on, love. It's time we went public with the fact that we're working as a team now, personally as well as professionally. Once the promotions within the agency are made public, there's no reason to keep our personal relationship under wraps. And I'll have to admit I'm getting impatient to make that announcement," he added, tightening his embrace and smiling down at her expectantly.

Suddenly confronted by the decisions she had been so studiously avoiding, Kate was overwhelmed by panic. Things were happening too fast; there were too many changes in her life for her to cope with. She wasn't ready to commit herself to the future Clint was depicting—not even in her work, much less in her personal life.

"I have to have more time to think about all of this," she said to Clint, pulling away from him. "I'm not ready to make such an important decision."

"You've had weeks to think about it, Kate," he said, clearly taken aback by her reaction. "I thought everything had already been decided."

"I hadn't realized you planned to change my job so drastically," Kate protested.

"We're not talking about your job," he exclaimed angrily. "We're talking about you and me. I've left you alone because I didn't want to cause problems for either of us at work. But I've made my feelings about you clear, Kate, and I'm not a patient man. I want to get on with our life together. Surely you can understand that."

"I guess I hadn't realized that you were serious in what you said—about us, I mean," Kate mumbled in consternation, not knowing what else to say.

"How much more serious can a man be than to ask a woman to marry him?" Clint cried out, acting more hurt than angry. "Maybe I haven't said it the way I should, but I love you, Kate. I want you to be my wife. When I said I wanted us to be a team, I meant that I wanted us to be partners in every way."

Kate was appalled at the thoughtlessness with which she had managed this situation. She had drifted along, avoiding its inevitability, giving no thought to Clint's feelings. Now she phrased a careful reply. "If I'm to be the partner you want, I have to be very sure of how I feel. I have to be certain I'm ready to commit myself to the kind of life you want. And for you and me, Clint, our work is a part of that life. And I've got to be certain that neither of us is making a mistake."

Clint regarded Kate intently, seeming to be making a decision himself. "I won't be kept dangling," he said. "Either you're with me all the way, or I've already made a mistake. I think you ought to be ready to give me an answer."

"For both our sakes, I have to be sure, Clint. I have to think carefully before I make a final decision."

He hesitated, and then nodded. "If you have any doubts, now's the time to deal with them. There won't be any turning back for either of us. Take the weekend to think things over, and call me when you've made up your mind. And Kate," he added in warning, "I'm going to make my announcement to the staff no later than Monday afternoon, regardless of what those announcements may be."

Kate nodded, understanding that he had issued an ultimatum. The moment for making her choice had come. "You'll have my answer by Monday morning," she told him. "And I promise that it will be one that we both can live with."

He gave her a long, searching look. "I hope it will be one that neither of us will regret."

CHAPTER 13

KATE SPENT FRIDAY EVENING in an agony of indecision. Everything she had worked for hung in the balance. She was being rushed along on a path that had been chosen for her by another. She was being forced to a decision she was not ready to make.

Yet Clint was right in saying you couldn't stand still. You had to grow. And if you moved on, it meant giving up part of the past—sometimes a part of it you loved. That was part of the price you paid for success.

And she was succeeding. The job Clint was offering her was the measure of her achievement. Some people worked all their lives and never reached that level of success. This was what a career was all about. It meant climbing as high as you could climb and reaping the rewards you had worked for. Clint was offering her the choice of going with him to the very top of their field. He was offering her the chance to realize the ambitions that had motivated her since she was old enough to dream about a career.

Somehow, though, she was no longer so sure about those ambitions. She had little enthusiasm for the new job Clint was proposing, and she certainly had to question the life she had been living lately. The constant round of parties and entertaining had grown ever more tedious. Too much of her time was being wasted on shallow, meaningless distractions, and with people whose values differed greatly from hers. Clint's priorities disturbed her, too. She had accepted the excesses, the clamor for status, as part of the price you paid for doing the work you wanted to do. But she seemed to be getting farther and farther away from the part of her job she enjoyed most. Ever more frequently, too, she found herself wondering whether she could be happy in a lifestyle based on values so different from her own.

Steve had said she needed to decide what she wanted out of life. At the time, she thought she knew. It had seemed simple enough to want to succeed in her work and be with the person she loved. But now she could see that there was something more to be considered. There wasn't only the question of *what* she wanted out of life; she had to decide *how* she wanted to live.

She was beginning to see, looking back on the happy times she had spent with Steve, that it had been the simplicity of their relationship that meant so much to her. She missed the contented hours they had spent at church together, the long walks and relaxing conversation, the sharing of their experiences, the uncomplicated pleasure of simply being together.

But those days were over. Steve had ended them. There was no point in hoping for something that could never be. She had to think realistically about the future, about the alternatives she now had to choose from. Clint had issued an ultimatum, and there would be no turning back from her decision. If she accepted the life he offered her, it would mean sharing the sophisticated fast-track life he had chosen for himself. If she refused his offer, it would mean the end of dreams she had nurtured since childhood. She would be turning down a professional opportunity that would likely never come her way again.

Whatever she decided, she had to resolve all uncertainties before she committed herself. She would be determining the path that she would follow for the rest of her life, and she had to be sure it was the right one.

For hours she pondered her decision. Several times she walked to the telephone, sorely tempted to call Steve. She needed so much to talk to him, to lean on his quiet, clearheaded wisdom. And yet each time she reached for the telephone, she was reminded that she no longer had the right to call on him.

Restlessly she paced the apartment searching for answers that didn't come, until finally, late Friday evening, it occurred to her that she did have someone to turn to. Someone who would understand, someone who could help her see things clearly. Picking up the telephone, she made a quick call, and then hurried to the bedroom and began packing a bag. In the morning she would be making a trip, one she should have made long ago. She was going to the person whose advice she could always depend on. She was going to talk to her father.

It was barely ten o'clock Saturday morning when Kate drove into the driveway at her parents' home. After she stopped the car, she sat for a moment looking at the familiar white frame house with its wide front porch and old-fashioned shutters. She felt the sting of tears as a wave of nostalgia swept over her. She had experienced the greatest contentment she had ever known in this peaceful house in this quiet little town, secure in the guidance of wise, loving parents. Here on this big front porch under the shade of these same tall maple trees, she had spent long, happy childhood hours drawing and coloring dresses for her paper dolls, acting out fairy tales, nursing a beloved puppy. It was here she painted the picture that brought her first recognition. It had been awarded first prize in the county art show, and no accomplishment of hers since had equaled the thrill of that achievement. How she had treasured that blue ribbon! Life had been so simple; it had taken so little to provide incalculable happiness.

The door of the house flew open in welcome then. Helen Logan hurried down the porch steps, John Logan followed close behind. By the time Kate had stepped from the car, her mother was standing beside her with outstretched arms waiting to clasp her in an embrace. Seeing the sparkle of pleasure in her mother's eyes and the delight in her father's smile, Kate had to fight to hold back the tears of joy she felt in seeing them. It was so fine to be with them once again. It was so very good to come home.

They spent a day of pleasant companionship, enjoying being together. Kate avoided discussion of her job, not wanting to mar her mother's pleasure by mention of her personal problems. It was late in the afternoon before she found the chance to be alone with her father. When, as was his custom, he announced that he wanted to take Kate's car out for a drive to see how roadworthy it was, she seized the opportunity to be with him.

As he drove, he made idle conversation, finally arriving at the outskirts of town. A few miles down the highway, he stopped at a roadside park, explaining that he wanted to inspect the engine. Kate climbed out of the car and waited until he finished poking among the wires and hoses to voice a timid request. "I'd like to talk to you, Dad. I badly need some advice."

"I thought maybe something might be troubling you, since you told us so little about yourself," he observed. "You know I'll help in any way I can."

"It's just that things are pretty muddled for me right

now, and I have to make an important decision I'm not sure I'm ready to make."

"About your job?"

"And about Clint. He has asked me to marry him, Dad, and I'm not sure what I want to do."

"The answer ought to be clear to you if you love him," her father said, regarding her soberly.

Kate turned away from him to stare at a nearby cluster of oak trees, not wanting him to see her reaction to his remark. "I'm not sure what love is anymore," she said finally. "I thought I loved Steve Turner, but it didn't turn out that way."

"Steve is the young doctor we met at church?"

Kate nodded. "We had a wonderful time for a while. But with the demands of his work and mine, we rarely had a chance to be together. He didn't—or wouldn't—understand how I feel about my career, and things didn't work out. It's over now." Kate hoped her father did not detect the regret in her voice.

"But do you love Clint, Kate?"

"He's a very attractive man, and I admire him. We work well together and share a lot of interests, but . . ." Kate's voice trailed away as she groped for a truthful answer.

John Logan looked up from the engine to cast a discerning glance at Kate. "It sounds to me as though you've got considerable doubts."

Kate leaned against the fender of the car, hesitating in her answer. "The trouble is that it's not just a matter of marrying or not marrying Clint. My career, everything I've worked for or thought I wanted, is tied up in this decision."

"Then I'd say this is doubly an important decision." John Logan's expression now mirrored his own concern.

"It is, Dad. That's why I needed to talk to you, to explain what all is involved. Coming all at once like this, it's a little more than I can handle on my own."

Her father wiped his hands on the cloth he had tucked in his hip pocket. Closing the hood of the car, he gave his full attention to Kate. "I think maybe you had better tell me more about this."

"It all happened when the agency got the Jason account," Kate began, plunging into her story. Relating the events of the past weeks, she poured out her concern about the promotion to Account Executive, Linda Grant's warning about Clint's ambitions, her own doubts about his business philosophy and the differences in their values, about the life she would be agreeing to lead. "I think I could know what I wanted to do if I were just deciding either about my job or about marrying Clint. But with both of them mixed together, I'm terribly confused. I realize there have to be changes in your work, as you go along. As you grow in your ability, you have to leave certain things behind you. I know you can't have everything in life the way you want it. It's just that I don't know whether I can adjust to so much change all at once."

"Then maybe you need to ask yourself whether you need to," her father commented.

"I have to make a choice, Dad. Clint wants an answer now. There's no going back to the way things were."

Her father fell silent, studying her with perceptive eyes. "I think, first of all, Kate, that you need to ask yourself what it is you want out of life," he said at last.

"Now you sound like Steve," Kate exclaimed impatiently. But that was another story that she had no desire to get into. Hurriedly she turned back to the problem she faced now. "I suppose I want what everybody wants," she said after a moment's thought. "I want to lead a successful life."

"Then I guess it comes down to what you consider to be a successful life," her father said gently.

Kate was perplexed by his comment. She sensed

that he was deliberately withholding his opinion. "That's what I'm trying to decide, Dad. That's why I want your advice."

He looked down at the ground, seeming to be turning something over in his mind. When at last he spoke, it was with a deep concern. "I could give you my opinion, Kate. I could tell you what I think you ought to do. But if I did, it wouldn't be your decision, and I don't think I have the right to tell you how you ought to live your life. That's a decision each one of us has to make on his own. It's not only our right but our responsibility. It's up to you to decide what to do with your life because it will be you who has to live with the consequences of your decision."

Kate looked at her father helplessly, deeply disappointed in his answer. "I know that, Dad. That's why I want your help so badly."

John Logan shook his head. A firmness came into his expression. "I can't tell you what you ought to do, Kate, but I think you know where to get the help you need to make your decision. You're not the little girl I raised, nor the fine young woman I know you to be if you don't know where to turn for guidance."

As Kate looked at him, perplexed, he placed a hand on her shoulder and squeezed it affectionately. "When you've had time to think about it, Kate, you'll see I've given you the best advice I can give you. And I think you'll also see what you need to do."

Kate's conversation with her father left her perturbed and uneasy, no closer to a solution to her problems. She was still distressed and confused the next morning when, following a lifelong custom, the Logan family made its weekly pilgrimage to church. Seated beside her parents in the little sanctuary where she had spent her Sunday mornings as a child, Kate felt a yearning for those carefree, uncomplicated times. Why couldn't life remain as simple as it had been then? Choices had seemed so clear and been so easy to make. She hadn't had to deal with the knowledge of human imperfection. Things were either right or wrong.

But then, John and Helen Logan had always made life seem simple and uncomplicated. They never seemed to struggle with questions of right or wrong. Looking at her parents, Kate felt envy. How wonderful it would be to know the commitment, the faith and trust they shared, their commitment to one another—and, it suddenly occurred to her, their commitment to God.

In that instant, Kate perceived with an illuminating clarity what her father had been trying to tell her. She felt as though a light had been turned on in a darkened room. With a certainty, she knew where she would find the answers she sought. She understood that she should look for help in the place the Logan family had always found it; she should turn to the source that had never failed them. For the answers she so sorely needed, she should turn to God.

Kate drove back to the city that afternoon with a firm objective. On the way to her apartment, she stopped by the church she and Steve had attended. Slipping into a pew at the back of the sanctuary, she sat for awhile absorbed in her thoughts. In the stillness of the empty chapel, she lost herself in prayer.

When she left the church at last, it was with an untroubled conscience and a certainty in her heart. Her choice was clear; her decision was made. And she knew that, whatever its outcome and wherever it might lead her, it was one she would never regret.

CHAPTER 14

ON MONDAY, KATE APPROACHED the day with a calm sense of purpose. Her resolve had not faltered; her decision was still clear. For better or worse, she knew she could live with it.

She was waiting in Clint's office when he arrived. He broke into a broad grin at the sight of her. "I'm glad to see you're as eager to get on with the show as I am," he said, holding his arms out to her. "Why don't we make the announcements first thing this morning and get the excitement over with so that people can get on with their work."

Kate couldn't help thinking how typical this reaction was of Clint. He was still taking it for granted that she had agreed to his proposal. She took a deep breath, bracing herself for what lay ahead. "We need to talk first," she said.

He set down his briefcase and walked to her side, pulling her close to him in a delighted embrace. "What is there to talk about? I think I know what you decided."

Kate stiffened and drew away from him. "Not

quite, Clint. We need to get things straight between us."

"I thought we had covered everything pretty thoroughly. You ought to know by now what we're looking at," he said in surprise.

"That's just it. I've had a chance to think, and I don't believe we look at things the same way, Clint."

His face clouded. "I don't know what you mean. We have the same ambitions, the same determination to succeed. And, while I haven't made a thing of it because I've never believed it a good idea to mix my business and personal life, I've come to care a great deal for you as a person. You're a beautiful, intelligent, desirable woman, Kate, and I want you to be my wife." He smiled indulgently at her. "It's really quite simple. I need you to make my life complete."

"But you haven't considered what I might need to make *my* life complete," Kate reminded him.

"I'm offering you everything a woman could want," he exclaimed. "I can give you success, social status, an exciting—quite a few women might say luxurious—lifestyle. We can go to the best places with the best people and make a name for ourselves in this city. And, in case this is bothering you," he added, a question seeming suddenly to occur to him, "you don't have to wonder whether there'll ever be any other women in my life. You know I'm far too much of a workaholic for that. You're the only woman I want or will ever need. With you working beside me, we can have it all."

Listening to Clint, seeing his intensity, Kate felt a painful regret. She understood that he was extending what, to him, was the greatest tribute he could pay to a woman. He was offering her the chance to share what he believed to be an ideal life. "Don't you see, though, that what we would have would be more of a business merger than a marriage," Kate said gently. "I admire you, respect your drive and your ambition.

You're an exciting person to be with. But I don't love you, Clint—not in the way a woman has to love a man to make him happy. And, even though you may want to believe you love me, you don't. Not really. If you did, you would have thought of marrying me long ago."

"Maybe I have taken you for granted in some ways, Kate. I'm not a man to make a fuss over a woman. But you've always been special to me. The woman I've included in everything I do, the woman I've spent all my time with. I thought you understood."

"I guess, like you, I've been too caught up in my work to think beyond it," Kate admitted. "But now that I have, I realize that you and I don't really want the same things, Clint. I'm not the woman you want, nor am I the woman you think I am. I want something far different out of life than you do."

"You're being ridiculous. Only a fool would turn down what I'm offering. What more could any woman possibly want?" Clint demanded, now angry.

Kate sighed, groping for a way to make him understand. She and Clint had been so close for such a long time. In his way, he had been very good to her, and there would be a void in her life without him. Most of all, she didn't want to hurt him. "I guess the thing is that I want *less*," she said at last. "I don't want the glitter and glamour, the pressure to stay ahead. I don't want to be better than everybody else. I just want to do the work I like to do and be with the people I like to be with. I guess I'm just not cut out for life in the fast track."

Clint paced a half turn about the room, glaring at Kate in disbelief. "I don't believe this. You must be out of your mind. I can name any number of women who would give anything to be in your place," he cried out, wounded pride now surfacing.

"I realize that. You're a very attractive man, and I'm very fond of you. It's just that we're not right for each other. I don't want to live the way you do. The things you want aren't important to me."

"You've never given me any indication that you felt this way," he accused her. "How could you have waited until now to do this?"

"You're right. I need to ask your forgiveness for that. I guess I haven't taken time for anything except my work. Things have been moving too fast for me to think about where I was going. But now that I've had time to think, I can see that I've been moving farther and farther away from the work I want to do and the way I want to live."

"You're not even making sense," Clint reproached her. "How could you possibly consider it to be a step backward when you've just been made Account Executive?"

"Because I don't want to be an Account Executive."

He gazed at her in disbelief. "Are you telling me you're turning down the promotion? Because if you are, I have to think you've lost your mind. Opportunities like this come along maybe once in a lifetime."

"But I liked the work I was doing. I was happier," Kate tried patiently to explain.

"Happy!" Clint sneered, throwing up his hands in disgust. "You're talking like an emotional, confused woman. What has happened to you, Kate?" He stopped suddenly and looked at her suspiciously. "This wouldn't have anything to do with this Dr. Turner you've been seeing, would it?"

Kate shook her head. "I'm not seeing Steve anymore. My decision has nothing to do with him. I've just realized that the life I've been leading isn't what I want."

"Then perhaps you'd like to tell me exactly what it is that you think you want," Clint said icily, his lips set in a tight, grim line.

"I would like to go on doing the job I was doing. I

like developing ideas, but I don't like going after accounts. I can't take the pressure of constant socializing. I have to have some time to think, some time for myself, some time to spend with people simply because I like them. I want time for a personal life apart from my job—for the spiritual side of my life. I guess what it adds up to, Clint, is that I'm not willing to have my whole life dictated by business considerations. There are other things that are important to me, too."

"Then I think you'd better look for a job at some other agency. There isn't any room here for laid-back people," Clint snapped. His eyes held an angry, antagonistic look, and his voice was cold and resentful. Kate knew she had offended him deeply.

"I understand that, Clint," she told him.

"You'd better. Because there won't be any turning back. I've made you an offer no woman in her right mind would refuse. If you don't accept it, there isn't a place for you here any more. Not at the agency and not with me."

"I know," Kate said sadly. "I realize that you don't understand my decision or my reasons for making it, and I want you to know that this is a very difficult thing for me to do. Your friendship means a great deal to me, and I owe you more than I'll ever be able to repay. You've taught me everything I know about this business, and I'll always be grateful to you. But we can't travel the same path, Clint, because we want to go in different directions."

He leveled a glance at her that had become hostile and threatening. "I hope you know what you're doing, because I don't intend to beg you to change your mind. It's all or nothing with you and me; that's the bottom line. If you walk out that door now, Kate, it's for the last time."

There was a chilling finality in his words, and a deep, aching sadness enveloped Kate. She had known she could not hope—did not want—to stay on at the agency. It would be an impossible situation for everyone. But she had hoped, had prayed, that she could somehow avoid this kind of enmity and misunderstanding.

In spite of Clint's reaction, though, her resolve did not waver. She did not regret her decision. "I'm sorry, Clint," she said softly.

He made no reply but stared at her with a long, recriminating gaze. Then he turned his back on her in contempt.

Looking at his rigid figure, Kate understood that there was nothing more to be said. Sadly, she left the office without looking back.

Kate spent the following day in a state of emotional suspension, unable to concentrate on the many decisions that lay ahead of her. She wandered about the apartment, plumping a sofa pillow, rinsing out a coffee cup, but finding no will to attempt any constructive task. She felt only an aching emptiness, a wrenching regret. Not at the decision she had made but at the shambles left in its wake.

Her confrontation with Clint had only confirmed her decision. Seeing him objectively, she now realized that she could never truly love him. His attraction for her had been only that of a successful, sophisticated man for an ambitious but inexperienced girl. Her admiration of him had been no more than the infatuation of an immature girl whose head was turned toward a superficial glamour. She had needed to learn for herself that his way of life could never be hers.

Not that Clint was dishonest or unethical. He was simply an opportunist, ready to turn every situation and any associate to his advantage. He was willing to make any concession to the standards of others necessary to benefit himself.

She could never live with that kind of insincerity—

or, for that matter, work with it. Nor would she ever be comfortable with Clint's personal values. She desired to live a life with Jesus as her guide and example. She knew now that before she considered marriage, her prospective mate must feel the same. She wanted a life and marriage like that of her parents, a life built on values they had no doubt about because those values came from their partnership with God.

The kind of life, she thought forlornly, that Steve Turner lived. He was a successful man with many demands made on him. Yet God was central in his life. She could see now what he had been trying to show her when he told her to decide what kind of life she wanted to live. He was trying to tell her that no achievement would bring happiness if it compromised your relationship with God.

Thinking back to the happy hours she had spent with Steve, she knew now with a heart-wrenching regret that this was what she wanted out of life. She wanted the serenity, the fulfillment of knowing she was living and working in the light of God's guidance and love.

At the thought, a faint glimmering of hope stirred in her mind. Perhaps she should tell Steve about her decision. Let him know that she had quit her job and was starting fresh.

But as quickly as it appeared, the hope vanished. If she called on Steve now, he would likely—being the person he was—offer her his support out of pity at this time when she so desperately needed it. And she didn't want Steve's sympathy; she wanted his respect. She had to prove to him that she was not only willing but able to act on her convictions and live by them, that she was able to manage her life successfully on her own. She had to get her life in order before she reached out to him. Her self-respect demanded it.

Dismally she surveyed the boxes of folders,

sketches, and a three-year collection of office bric-a-brac, which now littered the living room of her apartment. She had left the office yesterday morning without saying anything to her co-workers and had returned to the deserted offices last night to clear out her desk. She couldn't have borne the curious stares and unasked questions. The severing of her relationship with the agency was too abrupt and final.

Even today she still hadn't the will to begin unpacking the boxes. Her hurt was too painful, her wounds too fresh. The contents of the boxes were all that was left of three years of her life. All the associations, the accomplishments they represented were part of an as yet unevaluated past, a time in her life she had purposely ended and now had to put behind her. She had to concentrate on the difficult and uncertain future that lay ahead of her. If she had nothing else to show for the past three years, she at least had the wisdom gained from her mistakes. She knew what she wanted to do now. The problem would be whether or not she could succeed in doing it. Or, more exactly, finding the courage to set about doing it.

She spent the rest of the day trying to put the past behind her. She took a long walk in the park, refusing to dwell on memories of the times she had been there with Steve. The only chance there was of any future with him, however slight that chance might be, lay in her success in turning her life around. But a tiny spark of hope remained that gave her courage, that gave her the will to think of starting afresh.

By the next morning, she had mustered enough determination to try to sweep up the remnants of the past and go on. The first step was to unload the boxes in her living room and see what, if anything, could be salvaged from the last three years' work.

She had barely begun the distasteful task when the telephone interrupted. The call was from a distressed

Linda Grant. "You can tell me to butt out if you want to, but I've got to know what's going on," she began. "I hope we're good enough friends for you to know that I'm not calling to pass gossip but because of my concern. Is it true that you've left Clint Hansen's agency?"

"Do you mean the news is already out?" Kate said, dreading the repercussions of her decision but still resigned to them.

"The PR department at Jason Enterprises is in a panic, but Clint isn't giving out any news except to say that you aren't available. Our PR vice president is livid. He feels sure that Clint is deliberately withholding the facts from him. Maybe you think I'm out of line, and if you don't want to discuss this, I'll understand. But I care about you, Kate, and I want to help in any way I can. Naturally, anything you tell me will be confidential if that's the way you want it. Could we meet for lunch and talk?"

Kate hesitated, wondering if she was ready to talk about her sudden decision, even to Linda. Yet, sooner or later, she had to face the inevitable gossip, and she knew that Linda could be depended on to see that whatever information she passed along was true. "I guess I'm going to have to talk about it sometime. And I could use a little pepping up about now," she admitted.

"Come on down to the hotel, and I'll make sure that we have our talk in privacy. And, Kate," Linda added with emphatic sincerity, "I hope you trust me enough to believe that business hasn't got anything to do with my wanting to see you. I'm calling strictly as your friend."

Cheered by Linda's concern, Kate dressed quickly and was soon on her way. When she arrived at the hotel, she felt a keen loss. She was going to miss her association with Jason Enterprises. She had put a lot of herself into her work for them, and it would be difficult to see that work being developed by someone else.

Linda was waiting for her at a discreetly located table in a corner of the dining room. There was no pity in the broad smile with which she greeted Kate. Instead, not waiting for Kate to be seated, she said with obvious admiration, "I take it that the news is true. You really have walked out on Clint."

"Is that what the Jason people think?" Kate slipped into her chair, her brow furrowed. She was concerned by the suggestion that any of her former colleagues would mistakenly assume that she felt any ill will toward Clint.

"It's what I'm hoping. You deserve better." Linda's approval of Kate's decision was unmistakable.

"I hope you don't think there's any enmity between us—at least on my part," Kate said quickly. "Clint was very good to me. He taught me everything I know about this business. It's just that—" Her voice trailed off. How was she ever to explain?

Linda leaned forward in reassurance. "You don't have to talk about this if you don't want to. I didn't ask you here to pump you for information. I just thought you ought to know the reaction at Jason Enterprises."

"I'd like all of you to know that I have nothing against the Hansen Agency. In fact, Clint offered me a fine promotion. I'm sure most people will think I'm very ungrateful—if not completely demented—for turning it down." Kate took a sip of water from the crystal goblet the waiter had just filled. She waited until he had taken their order to resume. "I'm afraid I'm to blame, not Clint. I guess I'm a funny kind of duck, Linda, but I'm just not cut out for the competitiveness of this business. I just want to draw my little sketches and dream up my little ideas. And of course there's not much room for low-key people in this business." Kate shook her head ruefully as she finished, "No, Linda, it's not Clint or the agency that's lacking, it's me."

"Bosh!" Linda exclaimed impatiently. "All agencies aren't like Clint's. There's plenty of room for people with ideas and the talent to develop them."

"But few agencies are as successful as Clint's."

Linda buttered a roll and bit into it. "I won't argue Clint's success. He's not only aggressive in going after accounts, but he delivers a polished product. Nobody can fault him on performance. But everybody in the business knows how he drives the people who work for him. It's a wonder he can keep a staff at all."

"People work hard for Clint because he's exciting to work with. He's demanding, but he never asks you to work any harder than he does." Kate poked reflectively at the salad the waiter had served her and then shook her head. "Clint's not to blame for my leaving his agency, and I assure you the agency will get along very well without me."

"I hope the Jason PR vice president can be convinced of that," Linda commented. "It isn't any secret that it was your work that sold them on the account. I'm not sure how they're going to take the news that you won't be working on it."

"Clint has a very talented and capable team working on the Jason account. They won't disappoint you."

Linda fell silent, giving her attention to her salad. After a moment, she asked, regarding Kate thoughtfully. "What about you? Have you made any other plans?"

"Not yet. Obviously this was a difficult decision, and I haven't quite got a bearing on where I go from here." Kate toyed with a bit of lettuce. "I just want a quiet little job somewhere out of the spotlight where I can do the work I like to do. Of course, I don't know how good my chances are of finding one."

Linda regarded her steadily. "I know of at least one. Have you considered Jason Enterprises?"

Kate laid down her fork, dismayed. "Never, Linda. I wouldn't do that to Clint."

"I rather expected you wouldn't. But would you agree to let me pass the word around that you're available?"

"If you know of someone who's looking for a woman who doesn't work Sundays," Kate said with a grin.

"There are plenty of other people who won't, and don't you forget it. It's just a question of finding the right job," Linda assured her. She studied Kate for a moment. "Has this got something to do with your decision? The Sunday business, I mean."

"Partly. Mainly, though, I just didn't like the way my life was heading," Kate said candidly. "I guess what it comes down to is that I'm a Christian, Linda. And I couldn't be happy living any other kind of life."

"I'm glad to hear it," Linda said softly. "Because Mike and I have made the same decision. I thought at first that I was happier because Mike had come into my life, but we both soon realized that there was more to it than just having found one another. When we found out that we shared the same faith and wanted the same kind of life, our relationship took on a completely new dimension." Linda's eyes glowed as she expressed her thoughts. "I didn't think I could ever be this happy, Kate. And, I know, when you get things worked out—and they will work out—" she pronounced positively, "you'll look back and see that you've made the most important decision you'll ever make."

"I already know that." Kate's face clouded. "I only wish I had made it sooner."

Linda observed her closely. "Would this have anything to do with that young doctor you told me about?"

"A great deal," Kate admitted.

"Then tell him what you've done," Linda urged

her. Her lips curved in an impish grin. "If it were Mike, I know I'd never let him get away." Her smile faded then, and her eyes became serious. "And it will work out, Kate. I know it will. You've done the right thing."

Kate returned from her luncheon with Linda, her spirits lifted by the confidences they had shared, her day brightened by the knowledge that this special friend shared her Christian convictions. Encouraged, she was able to tackle the boxes with enthusiasm. By late afternoon, their contents had been sorted and stored away. Kate had even begun assembling a portfolio of her artwork and samples of her finished work. By Thursday morning, she wanted to be ready to go job-hunting.

As she worked, though, her thoughts kept returning to Linda's admonition about Steve Turner. She had to smile, thinking of Linda's determination. Even if he wanted to, Mike Donley wouldn't get a chance to change his mind. But her relationship with Steve was an entirely different matter. He had made it unmistakably clear that he was no longer interested in her.

But even if he wasn't, somehow she wanted him to know of her decision. If there was a chance that he still cared for her, even a little, she wanted to make the most of it. Because she knew, after talking to Linda, that her life couldn't move along until she knew without a doubt that there was no chance for her with Steve.

She debated calling him but decided against it. It would be too difficult to express herself in a telephone call. And she could hardly, out of the blue, invite him to dinner after so much time had gone by since she had seen him.

As she vacillated, a glimmer of hope appeared. Usually Steve could be found jogging in the park this time of day unless he had to make hospital rounds.

Grabbing up a sweater before she could weaken in her resolve, Kate headed for the park. If she walked long enough, there was a good chance of meeting up with Steve.

When she reached the park, she was strengthened in her decision. It was a beautiful fall afternoon, golden with autumn sunshine. An invigorating evening chill hung in the air, along with the smell of the falling leaves that littered the path. There was a pleasing satisfaction in feeling the crunch of the leaves beneath her feet, in feeling the sting of the breeze against her cheeks. It was wonderful to be alive, to be enjoying this beautiful day, to anticipate the possibility of seeing Steve.

Then, in an instant, the joy went out of the afternoon. Her hopes vanished. Her happy expectations disappeared at the same moment she found Steve. He was in the park just as she had hoped. She picked out his blond hair and tall figure instantly when she reached the tennis courts. But her anticipation turned to despair when she realized that Steve hadn't come to the park alone. His tennis partner was Rose Stanley, his pretty office nurse. And it was clear that they were having a wonderful time.

Kate stopped, transfixed by the sight. As she saw Rose's happy expression and heard the sound of her excited laughter, she felt a stab of pain. She was foolish to have thought a man as attractive, as desirable as Steve, would be sitting at home alone. Watching him enjoy himself with Rose, she felt a sick sense of longing. What a fool she had been to throw away something as wonderful as the relationship they had shared.

Crushed, she turned away and made her way desolately back to her apartment, fighting the bitter tears that blurred the path. Only now, when she had lost Steve, did she fully realize how very much she loved him.

CHAPTER 15

KATE DRAGGED HERSELF FROM BED the following morning feeling weary and defeated. Seeing Steve with Rose Stanley had been a heavy blow. She could see now that always, in the back of her mind, there had been the hope that he would want to resume their relationship when he learned of her decision to turn her life around. But, recalling the sight of him with Rose, she knew there could be no question about his feelings now. It was over between them. She had refused to make a place in her life for him when he wanted it, and now he had turned to somebody else.

She understood all too clearly why he might turn to Rose. Rose was not only a beautiful woman, she was an interesting, caring person who would be attractive to any man. It was only natural that Steve would turn to her and, inevitably, succumb to her winsome charm. Heavy-hearted, Kate faced the inescapable truth: her relationship with Steve was ended. She somehow had to find the will to make a life for herself without him. She had to pick up the pieces of her life and go on.

With a final, dispirited sigh, Kate put her unhappy thoughts aside and faced the morning. At least, she knew where to find the courage to meet an uncertain future. She was beginning her new life today in the only way she knew to go about it. She would put the mistakes of the past behind her and, with God's guidance, do her best to live this day as well as she could. With His help, she could face whatever was to come.

The first thing she had to do was find a job. And today was the time to start looking for one. Purposefully, Kate brewed a pot of tea and began a critical review of the samples of her work she had assembled in a portfolio, hoping they would convince somebody she was worth hiring. This morning she would start calling around to see what jobs, if any, might be available.

She had begun a list of business acquaintances she might contact for information when the telephone rang. She answered it to hear Linda Grant's enthusiastic voice. "I just turned up a lead on a job for you—something I think you would be really interested in."

"If it's a job, I'm interested in it," Kate said gratefully.

"Lacewell Associates is looking for a project director, and I can't think of anyone better qualified than you. And, Kate, although they aren't the biggest firm in town, I really think they're your kind of people."

Kate's spirits soared. The agency Linda mentioned was a small firm, but they had been in business for many years and had a reputation for dependability and honesty. If the job was anything close to what its title indicated, it might be exactly what she was hoping for.

"I told them of your experience and they're very eager to talk to you," Linda continued. "If you're interested, they would like to set up an interview with you."

With excited thanks to Linda, Kate hung up and put in a call to Lacewell Associates. Within minutes she had arranged for an interview that afternoon. She set out, portfolio in hand and a prayer in her heart, hoping this would be the opportunity she sought.

It was late afternoon when she returned to her apartment, weary but elated. She was now Project Director for Lacewell Associates, and more important she had gotten the job on her own terms. There would be no Sunday work or business entertaining. Her work would be strictly limited to project development. Best of all, the partners who headed the agency were indeed, as Linda had described them, very definitely her kind of people.

After making a call to Linda to express her gratitude, Kate spent the evening cleaning the apartment and mentally preparing herself to begin her new job. She tumbled into bed early, ready for a good night's sleep. But her last thought before she drifted off was a prayer of thanks. For the loyalty of a good friend and, more important, for the guidance she had received. She knew she could do it now, with God's help.

Kate went to work the next day. The agency was eager for her to begin. She left the office with a feeling of satisfaction. Her position at the agency was exactly as it had been described to her. The goals of the agency were ones she could support wholeheartedly. She felt sure she could accomplish something there that she could be proud of. She had made a good start on her new life.

Sunday morning found her seated in the sanctuary at church, fulfilling another vow she had made. This was the way she was going to begin every week from now on. Every Sunday, she would make a fresh start. She would put the mistakes and doubts of the past week behind and, seeking guidance, move on to the week ahead.

The service seemed to have special meaning for her this Sunday. Although she had come to church alone, she felt a comforting kinship with her fellow worshipers. After the service was over, she lingered to chat with some new acquaintances. It felt good to have shared this experience with them.

She was leaving the church when the moment came that she had dreaded. She had reached the foot of the steps at the entrance to the building when she saw Steve. She had purposely avoided looking for him during the service, but she had known that sooner or later they would have to meet. And now, meeting him face-to-face, she had to acknowledge him—along with the fact that he was here with somebody else. For, smiling up at him, was Rose Stanley, looking fresh and lovely and ever so happy to be at his side.

It took all of Kate's pride to meet Steve's gaze, to ignore his start of surprise. Forcing what she hoped was a pleasant smile, she greeted him politely and spoke briefly to Rose. But she limited her greeting to the fewest possible words before she hurried on to her car. She couldn't bear to let Steve discover how much it hurt her to see him with another woman.

Once at home, though, she gave in to the pain that stabbed her heart. As desolate as she had been before, she hadn't guessed how difficult it would be to face Steve. She hadn't imagined the pain of being reminded of the happy times they had shared—or the despair of knowing they would never share them again. Giving way to her hurt, she permitted herself to shed the tears that had been building within her over the past unhappy weeks.

But when her tears were finally spent, she felt a healing relief. In accepting the finality of her break with Steve, she found a bittersweet peace. She had endured the worst hurt of all and faced up to it. At least, she was moving on. And she had the consolation of knowing that she had set her feet on the right path, that with God's help she could make a good life for herself—even if she had to live it without Steve.

Subdued but resolute, Kate forced herself to pursue the plans she had made for the day. After lunch, she intended to take a long walk in the park and rid herself of her regrets and doubts. She couldn't look back; she had to go on. And she was determined to prove to herself that she could do it.

She forced down a sandwich and changed into jeans and a heavy sweater. She was ready to leave the apartment when the doorbell rang. Puzzled, she went to answer, unable to think of who might be calling on her. When she opened the door, her eyes widened in amazement. Clint Hansen stood outside her door.

Offering her a self-conscious half-smile, he said, "May I come in, Kate? I'd like to talk to you."

Kate stepped aside to invite him into the living room. He studied her uncertainly for a moment in silence. Finally, he blurted out uncomfortably, "We've got to put a stop to this ridiculous misunderstanding. We've got to get things back on track. I want you back, Kate, on whatever terms you name. We've accomplished too much together to throw it away."

Observing Clint's discomfiture, Kate couldn't help feeling a twinge of sadness. It was unlike him to humble himself to anyone like this. And, it was true, they had indeed accomplished a great deal together. The pity of it was that he would never understand why, to her, it represented a failure.

"We can't go back, Clint," she said gently. "It wouldn't work for either of us."

"I'm not asking you to marry me, Kate. I can see that you were right in refusing me. But that needn't interfere with what we can accomplish working together. As far as I'm concerned, we can just forget there was ever anything said about our personal lives. You can live yours, and I'll get on with mine." Clint relaxed noticeably, having dispensed with the personal area of their relationship. His glance sharpened, and his manner became businesslike as he moved on to what Kate perceived to be the real purpose of his visit. "If you don't like the sales part of the business, Doug can handle it and you can concentrate on development. We can set it up any way you like. But I need you, Kate—and I think, on reflection, you may be ready to admit that you need me. I think you'll concede that you aren't going to be able to find what I'm offering you at any other agency."

"As a matter of fact, I've already taken another job," Kate said, wishing fervently that Clint had spared them both this unhappy scene.

For an instant, a look of panic flickered in his eyes. But then, with a deprecating smile, he said, "I had no doubt that you could get a job, Kate, but I'm confident it won't measure up to what I'm offering you. May I ask what this fine new job of yours is?"

"I'm the Project Director for Lacewell Associates."

His lips curled scornfully. "Really, Kate. You can't be serious. That old-fashioned, small-time operation is going nowhere."

Goaded by his derisive dismissal of her new job, Kate rushed to the defense of her employers. "They have an excellent reputation, Clint. And, who knows? Maybe we'll come up with a new wrinkle or two."

Instantly, Clint's shoulders tensed. A belligerence appeared in the set of his jaw. "I hope you're not planning on taking any of the work you did for the Hansen Agency along with you. Because if you are, you'll find yourself in the middle of a nasty little lawsuit."

"I have no intention of doing anything like that," Kate said, stung by his accusation. "I understand that any work I did for you belongs to the agency."

"Then you should also understand that, under the

terms of our agreement with them, you're committed to developing the Jason account for the Hansen Agency." A fine line of perspiration beaded Clint's lips, and Kate recognized a nervous urgency in his words. It became suddenly clear to her that his visit to her today wasn't prompted so much by the fear of losing her as it was of losing the Jason account.

"I've already finished my work on the Jason account. You have only to work out the details, which I'm sure any number of people at the agency can do very capably," she reminded him.

"But there was an understanding that you would handle the account. You know that."

Kate returned his gaze calmly. "Jason Enterprises engaged the Hansen Agency, not me."

"But you were a part of the team, and now you're walking out on us because of a petty little misunderstanding. I never thought, after all I've done for you, that you would be vindictive toward me," Clint accused her in a change of tactic. Kate could see that he was playing on her conscience now, trying to make her feel that she had wronged him.

"You've done a lot for me, Clint, and I appreciate it. But I think I've repaid you with the work I've done for you," she said, refusing to be swayed. "You'll find a complete workup on the Jason account in my files, along with that of every other account I have ever worked on. I understand that all of it belongs to you, and I make no claim on it. And as far as taking my ideas with me are concerned, I give you my word that nothing I do for Lacewell will infringe on anything I did for you."

"You'd better make certain it doesn't, or I promise that you'll never work for another agency in this town again," Clint threatened, but Kate recognized a desperation in his voice.

"I don't want to be your enemy," she said softly. "And I promise that I will never use my work against you. In fact, I'm sure you'll agree that there's little chance of Lacewell Associates moving into competition with the Hansen Agency. They're like I am, Clint—a low-key organization of laid-back people who are satisfied to do what they like to do and do it well." She held out her hand in a gesture of reconciliation. "You should know that I would never work against you, Clint. I give you my word."

As he looked at her extended hand, Kate could see his belligerence turn to defeat. But he did not take her hand, and his stance remained stiff. "I hope you know what you're doing, Kate, because this is the last time I'll make you this offer."

"This is best for both of us, Clint," Kate said gently. "Sooner or later our association had to end."

He stared at her, uncomprehending, and after a moment turned away. Kate listened to the slam of the door sadly. What a pity it was that three years of association had to end in petty accusations. How much better it would have been if she could at least have retained some vestige of the admiration she had felt for Clint.

The sad thing was that she saw him at last for what he really was: a user, a shallow opportunist who had never really cared for her at all. She had to wonder if he would actually have married her. Her attraction for him had always been her work, which he had used to further his own career.

Kate felt no resentment toward him, only a sorrowful kind of pity. Clint would go on using people; he might even make a place for himself at the top. But what a price he would pay for it, how dear the cost to him would be. Kate saw now that his glib facade hid an insecure, fearful man who was dependent on the talents of others to reach a goal that he longed for with an insatiable hunger. No matter what heights of success Clint attained, he would never find any happiness. His goals were as flimsy as the foundation upon which they rested. Always, lurking behind him would be the fear of failure, a hated dependency on the talents of others.

For herself, Kate felt no fear of him. His threats were the impotent blusterings of a man who knew he had lost. Nor had she any fear of the future. She had confidence in her ability, and she now understood that there were plenty of people who did business with honesty and integrity. One man like Clint shouldn't be allowed to tarnish the image of the many successful people who didn't find it necessary to practice subterfuge and deceit. People like Linda Grant, businesses like Jason Enterprises. Theirs would be the true successes because they were built on honest work and fair dealing. All the qualities, Kate realized with a sorrowful finality, that Clint would never possess because he didn't understand them.

Feeling a need to erase the effects of her unfortunate scene with Clint, Kate set out on the walk that had been delayed by his arrival. From habit, her feet automatically set out toward the park across the street from her apartment complex.

As she walked in the park, she noted the signs of a season's ending. The trees were almost bare of leaves now, and the fall blossoms had faded. Squirrels scurried through banks of leaves, searching out nuts to add to the stores of food they were gathering in preparation for the advent of winter. Fall had produced its fruits, and they had been harvested. Following nature's plan, one season was giving way to another.

It occurred to Kate that she, too, was experiencing an ending. She had been tempered by experience and learned its lesson and was moving on to another stage in her life. There was a sadness in some of the things she was leaving behind her: the loss of an untested idealism, a regret for her mistaken pursuit of false goals, the emptiness she felt at the end of her relationship with Steve. But the future held no fear for her. She was ready to face it. With the strength of her rediscovered faith, she could meet the challenges that lay ahead. She had put the losses of the past behind her and was ready to get on with her life. It was dusk when Kate finished her walk and returned to her apartment complex. The entrance to her apartment was darkened by the deepening shadows, and at first she did not notice the figure seated on the steps outside her door.

But when he rose to his feet and spoke to her, there was no mistaking his familiar voice. "Kate?" he said, "I've been waiting for you."

CHAPTER 16

STEVE'S FEATURES WERE INDISTINCT in the shadows. Kate could not guess at his purpose in being here. But in her surprise at seeing him, she asked no questions.

"I was hoping you'd get home soon. Those steps were beginning to get hard," he said with a familiar little catch of humor in his voice. He rose from the steps and walked to the door with her. "I was hoping we could have a talk."

"Of course, Steve." She handed him her keys automatically. He unlocked the door for her, as had been his custom when he brought her home. Turning on the living room light, he stepped back for her to precede him into the room.

Nervously, she turned to face him, wondering what could have brought him here, her joy at his presence tempered by regret. Having him here so close to her only brought back painful memories of happier times.

He stood for a moment, watching her, his gaze tracing her features, lingering on each one in turn. "I came here to ask you a question," he said finally. "Why didn't you tell me you wanted to go to church this morning?"

"I guess because I didn't think it was important," she mumbled, pressed for a suitable answer, uncertain of the purpose of his question.

"Of course it was important. Surely you knew that if you were going to church, I would want you to go with me."

A faint ray of hope flickered in Kate's heart, only to be doused by the mental image of Rose Stanley standing close to Steve. "I really didn't think it mattered to you," she said, reacting to a wrench of jealousy. "You didn't seem to be in need of companionship."

A puzzled look flitted across his face. "You mean Rose?" he said in bewilderment. "Surely you didn't think . . ." He broke off in dismay. "Good heavens, Kate. Rose is just an understanding friend. Surely you knew that, all this time, I have only been waiting for a sign from you."

"No, I didn't," Kate retorted with aching pride. "You made it pretty clear that you didn't want anything more to do with me."

"How can you say that?" he exclaimed in exasperation. "All I asked for was one indication from you, one hint that you wanted to make time in your life for me."

"But you never called me. You never gave me a clue that you cared what happened," Kate protested. "I assumed that you considered yourself well rid of me."

"That's ridiculous, Kate." He regarded her with a hurt pride of his own. "I'll admit I wasn't going to hang around like a dog waiting to be thrown an occasional scrap from the table, but I never gave up hope that you would decide not to marry Clint."

"Marry Clint!" Kate cried out in frustration. "How could you think I would do such a thing?"

"He made it pretty clear how he felt about you." Steve's eyes accused her.

"I told you there was never anything between Clint and me, and I can assure you there never will be. As a matter of fact, I don't even work for him anymore."

His gaze became suddenly alert, intent. "What?"

"It means I've taken a new job. I'm Project Director at a small agency where I won't have to do all the entertaining I used to do, and I won't be working on weekends anymore. If anyone comes looking for me on Sunday morning, they'll have to come to church because that's where I plan to be." Kate watched anxiously for his reaction.

He took a step toward her, an intensity in his expression. "These changes you've made in your life, Kate," he said, his voice low and vibrant, "is there a place somewhere in them for me?"

"There is if you want it," Kate whispered, not daring to meet his eyes for fear she wouldn't see what she so desperately hoped for.

He took her hands in his and pulled her close to him. "You know this is all I've been waiting for. Just a sign, the slightest sign that you cared for me even half as much as I love you," he said, sweeping her up in a fierce embrace.

Kate's arms slipped around his neck and her lips moved eagerly to meet his in a longing, loving kiss filled with the pent-up feelings she could never with words have expressed. As they clung together, all doubt and misunderstanding vanished, swept away by the strength of their love.

He drew away at last and buried his face in her hair, holding her tightly in his arms as though he were afraid to let her go. "Oh, Kate. I thought I had lost you. It was hard to keep on hoping you'd come back to me."

"I thought you didn't want me," Kate murmured. "I saw you playing tennis with Rose, and then when you were together at church today, I thought you had found someone else."

"I'm sorry you thought that. Rose is the same kind friend she has always been, and she knows there could never be anyone else for me except you. I've loved you from that first day when you walked into my office. I've known from the beginning that you were the woman I had been waiting for. It just seemed that you hadn't time for anything except your career. I could only wait and hope that you would discover it wasn't enough for you."

"And I have discovered it, Steve," Kate told him earnestly. "I'll always love my work, but I see now that it's only a part of my life. There are other things that are far more important."

"Like me? And the way I feel about you?"

"Like you." She leaned back to regard him through eyes filled with love. "I know now what I want out of life. And I don't want any part of status-seeking and ruthless competition for wealth and success. I just want to do my job in a way I can be proud of and build the kind of life my parents have. I want what you and I had when we were together, Steve."

His eyes mirrored his delight as he pulled her close to him. "You can't know how I've longed to hear you say that, how many times I've prayed you would make this decision. But I couldn't force you into the lifestyle I'd chosen for myself. As much as I loved you, I had to wait for you to find your own way."

"And I have found it, Steve. I know exactly what I want. I want what you have. I want God to be a part of my life."

"Our life," Steve corrected, cradling her tenderly against him. With her cheek pressed to his chest, reassured by the strength of his arms, glorying in the warmth of his love, Kate felt a wonderful contentment. Feeling complete and fulfilled, she basked in the wonderful glow of feeling at one with Steve and knowing they were at one with God.

With a happy sigh, she drew away from him at last

and smiled up at him in invitation. "To prove how serious my intentions are, I'd like to make dinner for us tonight, Steve. I want you to see all the wonderful things I've learned to do with yogurt and bean sprouts."

His lips curved into a broad grin, and he shook his head. "It's very tempting, but I don't want my career wife-to-be spending her time in the kitchen on the night I propose to her. I have a much better idea. Why don't we go to Mama Carelli's, so that I can spread the good news when you say 'yes.'" A yearning appeared in his eyes. "That is what it's going to be, isn't it, Kate?"

"Oh, yes, Steve," Kate breathed blissfully. "And I can't think of a more perfect place to be proposed to than at Mama Carelli's."

He crooked his arm with a flourish and said with an inviting smile, "Then shall we be on our way, Miss Logan?"

Kate tucked her arm in his and replied, "By all means, Dr. Turner."

And as they set out together, there was a magic in the evening, a glow as dazzling as the millions of stars that twinkled in the sky. Their hopes for the future were as bright, their faith in each other as limitless as their certainty in God's promise to those who choose to walk with Him.

ABOUT THE AUTHOR

MARILYN AUSTIN lives in Dallas, Texas. Now that her children are grown, she is a full time writer and has published nine books. Marilyn is inspired by people who successsfully meet life's challenges, whether prompted by career, personal adversity, or an unusual experience. It is her conviction that people with strong religious faith can better cope with whatever problems they may be confronted with. We are faced with decisions daily, and a strong faith can make those decisions easier. It is this message that Marilyn hopes to convey to her readers.

A Letter To Our Readers

Dear Reader:

Welcome to the world of Serenade Books—a series designed to bring you the most beautiful love stories in the world of inspirational romance. They will uplift you, encourage you, and provide hours of wholesome entertainment, so thousands of readers have testified. In order that we might better contribute to your reading enjoyment, we would appreciate your taking a few minutes to respond to the following questions and return to:

Editor, Serenade Books
The Zondervan Publishing House
1415 Lake Drive, S.E.
Grand Rapids, Michigan 49506

1. Did you enjoy reading LOVE MORE PRECIOUS?
   - ☐ Very much. I would like to see more books by this author!
   - ☐ Moderately
   - ☐ I would have enjoyed it more if ________________

2. Where did you purchase this book? ________________

3. What influenced your decision to purchase this book?
   - ☐ Cover
   - ☐ Title
   - ☐ Publicity
   - ☐ Back cover copy
   - ☐ Friends
   - ☐ Other ____________

4. What are some inspirational themes you would like to see treated in future books?

____

5. Please indicate your age range:

- ☐ Under 18
- ☐ 18–24
- ☐ 25–34
- ☐ 35–45
- ☐ 46–55
- ☐ Over 55

6. If you are interested in receiving information about our Serenade Home Reader Service, in which you will be offered new and exciting novels on a regular basis, please give us your name and address. (This does NOT obligate you for membership.)

Name ______________________________

Occupation ______________________________

Address ______________________________

City ______________ State ____________ Zip ____________

Serenade/Saga books are inspirational romances in historical settings, designed to bring you a joyful, heart-lifting reading experience.

Serenade/Saga books available in your local book store:

#1 *Summer Snow*, Sandy Dengler
#2 *Call Her Blessed*, Jeanette Gilge
#3 *Ina*, Karen Baker Kletzing
#4 *Juliana of Clover Hill*, Brenda Knight Graham
#5 *Song of the Nereids*, Sandy Dengler
#6 *Anna's Rocking Chair*, Elaine Watson
#7 *In Love's Own Time*, Susan C. Feldhake
#8 *Yankee Bride*, Jane Peart
#9 *Light of My Heart*, Kathleen Karr
#10 *Love Beyond Surrender*, Susan C. Feldhake
#11 *All the Days After Sunday*, Jeanette Gilge
#12 *Winterspring*, Sandy Dengler
#13 *Hand Me Down the Dawn*, Mary Harwell Sayler
#14 *Rebel Bride*, Jane Peart
#15 *Speak Softly, Love*, Kathleen Yapp
#16 *From This Day Forward*, Kathleen Karr
#17 *The River Between*, Jacquelyn Cook
#18 *Valiant Bride*, Jane Peart
#19 *Wait for the Sun*, Maryn Langer
#20 *Kincaid of Cripple Creek*, Peggy Darty
#21 *Love's Gentle Journey*, Kay Cornelius
#22 *Applegate Landing*, Jean Conrad
#23 *Beyond the Smoky Curtain*, Mary Harwell Sayler
#24 *To Dwell in the Land*, Elaine Watson
#25 *Moon for a Candle*, Maryn Langer
#26 *The Conviction of Charlotte Grey*, Jeanne Cheyney
#27 *Opal Fire*, Sandy Dengler
#28 *Divide the Joy*, Maryn Langer

#29 *Cimarron Sunset*, Peggy Darty
#30 *This Rolling Land*, Sandy Dengler
#31 *The Wind Along the River*, Jacquelyn Cook
#32 *Sycamore Settlement*,
Suzanne Pierson Ellison
#33 *Where Morning Dawns*, Irene Brand

Serenade / Serenata books are inspirational romances in contemporary settings, designed to bring you a joyful, heart-lifting reading experience.

#30 *Heart Aflame*, Susan Kirby
#31 *By Love Restored*, Nancy Johanson
#32 *Karaleen*, Mary Carpenter Reid
#33 *Love's Full Circle*, Lurlene McDaniel
#34 *A New Love*, Mab Graff Hoover
#35 *The Lessons of Love*, Susan Phillips
#36 *For Always*, Molly Noble Bull

Watch for other books in both the *Serenade/Saga* (historical) and *Serenade/Serenata* (contemporary) series coming soon.